This book should be returned to any branch of the
Lancashire County Library on or before the date shown

2 9 JUN 2015

SAL

10 Dec

- 3 DEC 2018

By Ellie Boswell

THE WITCH OF TURLINGHAM ACADEMY
UNDERCOVER MAGIC
SECRETS AND SORCERY
BOX OF TRICKS
SPELLBOUND

THE WITCH OF
TURLINGHAM ACADEMY

SPELLBOUND

ELLIE BOSWELL

LITTLE, BROWN BOOKS FOR YOUNG READERS
www.lbkids.co.uk

LITTLE, BROWN BOOKS FOR YOUNG READERS

First published in Great Britain in 2013 by Little, Brown Books for Young Readers

Copyright © 2013 by Working Partners

The moral right of the author has been asserted.

A CIP catalogue record for this book
is available from the British Library.

ISBN 978-0-34900-147-0

Typeset in Minion by M Rules
Printed and bound in Great Britain by
Clays Ltd, St Ives plc

Papers used by LBYR are from well-managed forests
and other responsible sources.

MIX
Paper from
responsible sources
FSC® C104740
www.fsc.org

Little, Brown Books for Young Readers
An imprint of
Little, Brown Book Group
100 Victoria Embankment
London EC4Y 0DY

An Hachette UK Company
www.hachette.co.uk

www.lbkids.co.uk

With special thanks to
Leila Rasheed

ONE

Sophie hurried across the courtyard in front of Turlingham Academy, clutching a gold-wrapped present and a white envelope. It was the last day of the Christmas term, and the drive was crowded with cars. Parents and children squealed as they saw each other for the first time in months, and the cold air rang with shouts of 'Mum! Dad!' and 'How you've grown!' Sophie grinned to herself – school was great, but she knew how lucky she was to live with her parents on the grounds. She loved seeing everyone so happy as they hugged their families again.

Above her the leafless tree branches shivered, and gulls wheeled around the turrets of the ancient school building. Sophie craned right and left, trying to spot Ashton Gibson. She'd already looked in the boys' dorms, and tried to find Katy to see if she knew where he was. Katy was Ashton's sister, not to mention Sophie's best friend, so she would know how important it was for Sophie to find him.

But in all this excitement it was like looking for a specific raisin in a Christmas cake. She clutched the present tighter. What if he didn't like it? Oh, but he had to! She was sure he would ... but then, she'd never bought a present for a boyfriend before – never even had a boyfriend before. It still didn't seem real that she was going out with the best-looking boy in Year 10.

She took out her phone and rang Katy, smiling as the picture of her best friend pulling a stupid face came up on the screen. Katy's phone rang twice and then, in the middle of a ring, it switched to voicemail.

'Hey, this is Katy, I can't answer the phone right now, leave a message!'

Sophie hung up before the beep. *Must be on silent,* she thought. *Typical!*

'Sophie!' called a familiar American voice.

She turned round. Erin, Lauren and Joanna were waving at her from under the big old oak tree where they usually hung out. Sophie ran over.

Erin held out her arms for a hug. 'I guess I'd better say, "Happy Christmas". In case I don't see you again.'

'But aren't you leaving tomorrow?' Sophie hugged her.

Erin nodded. 'The flight's first thing in the morning. But I thought I would say it now, just in case – you know how crazy the last day of term always is.'

'So, is that for Ashton?' Joanna asked, looking at the card and the gold-wrapped parcel Sophie was holding.

Sophie blushed and laughed. 'Yeah, it's the new Jareth Quinn film. I hope he likes it.'

'Of course he will!' Lauren's eyes sparkled. 'I wonder if he'll kiss you when you give him his present—'

'He better!' Erin said. 'I'd kiss someone if they gave me Jareth for Christmas.' Everyone laughed.

'What do you think he's got *you*, Sophie?' Joanna asked.

'I don't know. Maybe nothing.' Sophie blushed again. 'And that would be fine ... I just don't know what to expect.' Sophie looked around for him again. 'But I still can't find him. Or Katy, for that matter.'

'Oh, I saw them from the window about five minutes ago,' Lauren said. 'They were by the gate.'

'Brilliant!' Sophie gave a hop of relief. 'Thanks, Lauren.'

She left her friends and ran along the drive towards the entrance to the school ground. She was buzzing with anxiety to see Ashton and Katy – and not just because they were two of her favourite people in the world. There was a lot going on that she couldn't tell Erin and the girls. She was a witch, Ashton and Katy were witch hunters – and there was a whole secret world of witches and witch hunters who were very, very unhappy because they were friends. So unhappy that they'd driven Katy and Ashton's parents into hiding. Sophie ached to think how worried her friends must be about them.

She came up to the big wrought-iron gates that marked the entrance to the school grounds. Mr McGowan was there, talking to some Turlingham boys.

'Mr McGowan,' Sophie began breathlessly as she reached him, 'have you seen Ashton or Katy anywhere?'

'The Gibsons?' Mr McGowan hesitated as the boys walked away. An odd expression drifted across his face, as if he was trying to call up an old memory. Then his face cleared. 'You've missed them, I'm afraid. They've already left.'

Sophie stood staring at him with her mouth open. *Left? Without telling her? Without even saying goodbye? Or Happy Christmas?*

'So early?' she managed finally. The card in her hand drooped. Was this what it felt like to have your heart broken by your first boyfriend? Ashton hadn't even bothered to stick around and wait for five minutes.

Mr McGowan nodded, looking at her sympathetically. 'There must have been a change of plan,' he said slowly, seeming a little confused.

'Change of plan?' Sophie didn't understand.

'Their uncle came to pick them up ...' Mr McGowan sounded more confident with every word.

For a second, Sophie thought she had misheard. She *hoped* she had misheard. 'Uncle?'

'Yes,' he replied, 'their uncle *Robert*.'

Sophie's breath came fast and she hardly heard his words.

'Sophie? Sophie, are you OK?'

He couldn't have said Robert. Not *Robert*. That was impossible ... because the last time she'd seen Katy and Ashton's uncle Robert, he'd been trying to kill them all! He had even possessed Sophie's father's fox familiar and sworn revenge.

'Are you sure his name was Robert?' she asked, still praying she had misheard.

Mr McGowan nodded. 'Positive.' A slight frown flitted over his face. He added, 'He said how wonderful it was to see them again and how he'd missed them. Seemed like a nice man.'

Sophie's mind whirled. Yes – their uncle Robert Lloyd did seem like a nice man. That was, if you didn't know he was a homicidal maniac! He hated witch hunters because they had driven him out of the community after he married Sophie's aunt Angelica. If Katy and Ashton were with him they were in grave danger.

Sophie spun round, looking wildly for her mum and dad. She spotted them on the far side of the courtyard, talking to a group of parents. Sophie raced over to them and tugged her dad's sleeve.

He looked down, startled. 'Soph? What is it?'

'I've got to talk to you,' she whispered. 'Both of you. Now!'

Her mother looked annoyed. 'We're in the middle of a conversation, Sophie. This is not very polite—'

'*Now*, Mum!' Sophie hissed. She brought her two thumbs together to make a W, hoping her mother would understand that this was witch business. From the look on her face, Sophie knew the message had got through.

Her mother quickly hid her shocked expression and smiled politely at the parents. 'Please excuse us ...'

Sophie pulled her parents across the courtyard towards Mr McGowan.

'It's Katy and Ashton,' she said as soon as she was sure no one could overhear. 'They've gone. Mr McGowan says they left with their uncle Robert!'

'What?!' her mum and dad exclaimed at the same moment.

Sophie nodded, fear bringing tears to her eyes. Her parents looked at each other in horror. Sophie's mum was the first to find her tongue.

'There must be some mistake. We have very strict rules about that kind of thing. Mr McGowan would never have let them go with someone who wasn't their parent!' She broke into a run, heading towards Mr McGowan, and Sophie and her father followed.

Mr McGowan was standing where Sophie had left him, an expression of vague, pleasant puzzlement on his face. Sophie thought he looked spaced out – but then, that was Mr McGowan for you.

'Sophie says you let Katy and Ashton go with someone who claimed to be their uncle?' Sophie's mother burst out as she reached him.

'That's right.' Mr McGowan smiled.

'How could you do such a thing?' Sophie had never heard her mum sound so angry. 'You know perfectly well that's against school protocol. What proof have you got that this man was who he said he was?'

She didn't wait for an answer as she pulled out her mobile phone and began dialling.

Sophie caught her hand. 'Are you calling the police?'

'Of course!' she replied. 'There is no time to lose.'

Sophie didn't know if this was a good idea or not. 'But what if this is about witches and witch hunters?' she whispered so Mr McGowan couldn't hear.

Sophie's dad looked at Sophie. 'It's about two children going missing, Sophie. That comes first.'

Sophie felt a sick churning in her stomach. She knew their uncle would do anything for revenge on the witch hunters who'd separated him and Angelica. Even hurt his own nephew and niece. Her mum was right, this was something they needed to get the police involved in. They had to do whatever it took to get Katy and Ashton home safe.

'Police, please. I need to report two missing children.'

Mr McGowan cleared his throat. 'But ... but it's OK.' He sounded genuinely puzzled. 'The parents sent a letter saying that it was OK for their uncle to pick them up.'

He drew a folded piece of paper out of his pocket. Sophie's dad snatched it, and Sophie stood on tiptoe to read over his arm.

It was just a couple of type-written sentences, without even a signature. It could have been written by anyone! What had got into Mr McGowan?

Sophie's mum glanced at the letter. 'Oh, I see. Well, that's OK then. The letter explains it all,' she said in a monotone voice. To the person on the phone, she added. 'Sorry to bother you. It was a misunderstanding.' She flipped her phone shut and smiled at them all. 'It all makes perfect sense. Of course their uncle would pick them up, given the circumstances.'

Sophie looked at her in disbelief, and then at her father, who was frowning thoughtfully. Were they reading the same letter?

'Yes, that's what I thought as soon as I read it,' Mr McGowan said, smiling too. 'It all makes perfect sense.'

'But what about the protocol?' Sophie asked. 'Are you serious, Mum?'

'Oh, protocol.' Sophie's mum gave a light laugh. 'We teachers fuss too much, that's what I think. The kids will be fine.'

Sophie's mum would never say that! Sophie stared at the letter, then turned to her dad. She was about to beg him to look properly at the letter, but he put a hand on her shoulder.

'Oh, isn't that your friend Lauren's parents? We must go and say hello!' he said, and gently pushed Sophie away from the gate.

'Dad!' Sophie complained. What was he doing? But then she looked up and caught his eye as he winked at her. *Oh – I see. Not in front of the History teacher . . .* He steered her behind a bush and took the letter from her with a frown.

'Yes, I thought so. The paper's been treated with a spell,' he said quietly, looking down at the letter. 'It's what we call a blind. It makes whatever's written on it extremely persuasive to humans. A simple trick. Luckily, it's easy to reverse. Watch this.'

Sophie's father bent and picked up an icy leaf from the ground. He shook the ice on to the paper and let it melt there into crystal clear drops of water.

'Powers of the Earth – earth, water, wind and fire,' he said. A ray of winter sun caught the pocket watch he always wore, his Source. It glinted as if it were a winking golden eye. 'Melt this spell away like ice.'

Sophie saw no difference in the letter, but Sophie's father walked purposefully back to the gate and held the paper out to Mr McGowan and her mother.

'So you're both quite sure this letter explains everything?' he said with a raised eyebrow.

Mr McGowan studied the writing, then did a double take. Sophie's mum went pale with shock.

'Oh my goodness!' she exclaimed.

Mr McGowan looked around wildly. 'I ... the man was here a moment ago. He said he was their uncle. It all seemed to make sense at the time ... and *you* said there was no reason to worry, headmistress.'

'I did?' Sophie's mum put a hand to her mouth. 'I did. I remember. But why would I say that?'

'And I just let them go!' Mr McGowan looked distraught. 'I don't get it. I would never ... if anything happens to them ... '

'We must call Katy and Ashton's parents,' Sophie's mother interrupted. 'I have their number in my office ... '

Sophie opened her mouth then closed it again. She knew the Gibson parents wouldn't be answering. They weren't at home, they were on the run from the witch hunters. And they'd got rid of their mobiles so they couldn't be traced.

'Er ... ' She looked at Mr McGowan, who was biting his lip anxiously as he dialled the police. She couldn't talk about witch business in front of her History teacher. 'They ... they don't have mobiles, remember, Mum?' she said, hoping her mother would get the hint and remember the Gibsons' situation.

Sophie's mum had gone so white it was clear she *did* remember. 'Oh goodness ... ' she whispered under her breath. 'Yes, the Gibsons are ... having phone trouble,' she explained to Mr McGowan. 'I don't think we can contact them.'

Sophie listened as her History teacher explained this to the police and then hung up.

'They're on their way,' he said.

A tense silence fell as Sophie, her mum and dad and Mr McGowan all looked desperately towards the big wrought-iron gates, hoping the police would arrive soon. Sophie tried to call Katy again, but this time it went straight to voicemail.

That's not a good sign . . .

'Katy, if you get this, call me, like right now. OK?' she said after the beep. She wanted to say more – that Robert wouldn't get away with this, that she wasn't going to let anything happen to her. But what if it was Robert at the other end, and not Katy?

Sophie's heart beat hard in her chest as she dialled Ashton's number.

'This is Ashton. Leave a message!'

Sophie hesitated, holding her breath. Then she hung up.

She was still staring at the phone when she heard

a car engine on the drive. She looked up, expecting to see a police car. Instead, Sophie saw an ancient-looking white car, covered in rust patches, coming along the school drive. In the front seats were a man and a woman wearing sunglasses. Sophie briefly thought that it was odd they were wearing sunglasses in the middle of winter. As the car approached them, the woman leaned out of the window and took her sunglasses off.

'Mrs Gibson!' Sophie cried after a second. She barely recognised her. Usually Katy's mum was so glamorous and groomed, despite the scar on her face. But now she seemed exhausted. She had wrinkles that Sophie was sure hadn't been there the last time they'd seen each other.

Mr Gibson stopped the car and got out. Sophie couldn't return his eager smile. She felt sick.

Her mother stepped forward. 'Mr Gibson, Mrs Gibson.' Her face was pale, but she went on. 'I'm sorry to tell you that Katy and Ashton have gone.'

Mr and Mrs Gibson looked at each other, as if expecting the other to know what she was talking about.

'A man calling himself their "Uncle Robert" came and took them away.'

Mr Gibson went white. Mrs Gibson gasped.

'We're still trying to understand how it can have happened. I'm so, so sorry.'

'How could you do this? How could you let them go with him?' Mr Gibson burst out. He paused, evidently trying to get a grip on himself. 'If that man harms them—'

'I think I may faint,' Mrs Gibson could barely speak; she reached out to steady herself on the car. Sophie's mother quickly moved to support her.

'I'll bring you a glass of water,' Sophie said, desperate to help.

Mr Gibson didn't seem to have even heard her. 'We've got to find them. We've got to find them this minute.' He got back into the car and turned the key. The engine revved. Mrs Gibson, still holding on to the car to support herself, staggered back to her seat.

'Mr Gibson! Wait!' Sophie's mother hurried after them and held the door open. 'The best thing you can do is stay here and wait for—'

'While our children are missing? Never!' Mr Gibson leaned over and slammed his wife's door. The car jerked forward, with a screech of tyres, trying to escape the car park. Sophie's parents stared in shock. Children and parents scattered as Mr Gibson reversed. The engine stalled.

Sophie ran to the car and leaned in through the open window. She could hear a police siren in the distance, coming closer. Mr Gibson swore as he tried to restart the engine.

'Don't go,' she begged. 'We've already called the police, they'll be here any moment, they'll want to talk to you.'

'The police?' Mrs Gibson's terrified expression made Sophie's skin crawl.

'We have to go. NOW!' Mr Gibson turned the key again and the engine burst into life.

'What? Why?' Sophie exclaimed over the revving. 'The police can help us find them!'

Mrs Gibson turned to Sophie. But all she said, her voice shaking, was. 'Don't tell the police you saw us. Please!'

'Why not?' Sophie demanded. Why were the Gibsons so afraid? 'Are you in trouble?'

'We haven't time to explain,' Mr Gibson told her. 'Just please don't say you saw us. We'll look for Katy and Ashton, and we'll let you know as soon as we find them.'

The car screeched forward, and Sophie jumped back as gravel sprayed her shins. The Gibsons' old car drove with lumbering haste down the drive towards the gates. Sophie could only stare after them.

She blinked as blue lights reflected off the tree trunks and a siren split the air. A police car drove through the gates. The students stared, some excited, others frightened. Sophie gulped – the police car was heading straight for the Gibsons. There was no way they wouldn't see them.

She ran back to her parents.

'Dad, you've got to do something to stop the police seeing them!' she whispered.

To her relief, her father didn't ask for an explanation. He simply nodded, backed away from her mum and Mr McGowan and bent to scoop up a handful of slushy ice from a puddle. He tossed it into the air.

'Forces of the Earth,' he muttered, 'bring the winter.'

His pocket watch glinted. There was a blast of bitter wind and the temperature sank by several degrees in an instant. The children, parents and teachers looked up and around, shivering in surprise. The sky darkened, and suddenly a blizzard was whipping its icy tail all around them.

'Snow!' Erin squealed, jumping up to catch the drifting flakes. Others ran for shelter. Mr McGowan rubbed his arms, looking confused as he muttered something about global warming.

'Oh how weird,' Lauren cried out, pointing, 'it's only on that side of the road.'

The snow rolled like a white wave between the police car and the Gibsons' car, hiding the Gibsons from the police. Sophie was shivering so hard her teeth were chattering, but she couldn't help feeling impressed by her father's powers. As the Gibsons drove out of the gates and the police car pulled up in front of the school, she prayed that the Gibsons would be able to find Katy and Ashton, but she knew she couldn't just leave them to it – she had to do something, anything, to stop Robert Lloyd. He had her best friend and her boyfriend in his clutches, and Sophie wasn't going to rest until she got them back.

TWO

Sophie huddled with Erin, Kaz, Lauren and Joanna on the sofa in the Year 11 common room. She'd so often wished they were allowed in here – the Year 11s had a pool table and a DVD player and everything. But now they were here, it was for all the wrong reasons. Erin was completely silent for the first time in Sophie's memory. Joanna kept sniffing back tears, and Lauren and Kaz were quiet and shocked. The three police officers standing around by the door looked very serious. When she looked at their unsmiling faces, Sophie wanted to cry. This wasn't a mistake, it wasn't a nightmare. Her best friend and her boyfriend had been kidnapped.

She looked up as Callum and Oliver came in, followed by Mrs Freeman and a couple more of the boys from Ashton's year. Callum looked as stunned and sick as she felt. Sophie's stomach churned. How could she have forgotten about Callum? He must be as worried about Katy as she was about Ashton. Callum caught her eye and gave her a small smile. He came to sit on the arm of the sofa next to her.

Mrs Freeman shut the door and turned to the police officers. 'These are Katy and Ashton's closest friends,' she said. Her voice had lost its usual sharpness.

'Thank you.' The oldest policeman steepled his fingers and looked at the silent group in front of him. 'As you have been told, Katy and Ashton Gibson were picked up from school at approximately 3.30p.m. by a man who claimed to be their uncle Robert. But we haven't been able to contact either of them, so we need to ask you some questions.' The older policeman nodded at the policewoman. She looked more nervous than he did. She cleared her throat.

'Have any of you noticed anything strange about Katy's and Ashton's behaviour recently?'

There was silence. Sophie looked around. It seemed no one was sure how to answer.

'You aren't in any trouble, you know,' the policewoman said gently.

'It doesn't feel like it!' Erin whispered in Sophie's ear.

Sophie had to agree. The way they were lined up in front of the police officers, it felt as if they were being interrogated. She knew she had to be careful not to give away anything about Mr and Mrs Gibson – she still didn't understand why they were scared of the police, but she couldn't forget the look on Mrs Gibson's face. She was determined to keep Katy's parents' secret.

'We all just want Katy and Ashton to be safe,' the policewoman went on. 'Even if they went of their own accord, they are still in danger until we know where they are and can help them. Did they ever talk about running away?'

This one was easy. Sophie found her voice. 'No, never.'

'So they were looking forward to going home for the holidays?'

Sophie nodded. Then she remembered, they wouldn't have been going home, they would have gone with their parents – wherever they were hiding out while they were on the run from the witch hunters. She knew her expression looked guilty, and she could see that the police officers had spotted it. The older man and the younger one exchanged a glance.

'So you all say they have been behaving normally?' the young policeman asked.

Kaz spoke, making Sophie jump. 'Well … not exactly *normally*.'

Kaz's words seemed to encourage the others to speak. Erin joined in, 'Katy was being really weird last week, actually.'

'It was like she was a different person!' Joanna agreed.

Sophie winced. She *had been* a different person! She'd been possessed by the mischievous ghost of an ancient witch. But she couldn't tell the policeman that.

'Weird, how?' the policewoman asked.

24

The girls looked at each other.

'Just . . . angry all the time,' Lauren said. The others nodded.

'*Really* angry,' agreed Joanna.

'Yeah,' said Erin. 'She didn't want to hang out with us any more.'

'But she came around after a while,' Sophie reminded them. 'She was normal in the last couple of days.' She wished she could tell all her friends that it wasn't Katy's fault she'd been so weird.

The police officers exchanged meaningful glances. The policewoman wrote something down on a pad of paper.

The older policeman spoke directly to Callum. 'You're her boyfriend, I hear. Surely she confided in you?'

'Well yes . . . but n-no. Nothing about this.' Callum looked haunted. Sophie knew he knew about the witches and witch hunters. He probably wasn't sure how much he could say without putting Katy and Ashton in even more danger. There was an uncomfortable silence.

'Something troubling her at home?' the police-woman said. 'Family problems perhaps? How was her relationship with her parents?'

'Not good!' said Erin at once. 'They hardly ever called her. And she used to say she didn't like how much pressure they put on her.'

The others nodded and agreed. Sophie didn't know what to say. Things were very different between them now, but all this didn't make the Gibson parents look good. The older policeman scribbled something on a pad of paper.

'And their uncle Robert Lloyd,' said the police-woman. 'Have you ever met him before? Do you know anything about him?'

'Um . . . ' Oliver frowned. 'Didn't he used to work in the old people's home?'

There was a chorus of agreement. Sophie wanted to groan. She'd hoped people had forgotten that. Then Kaz sat forward eagerly. 'Sophie, isn't your grand-mother in there? Maybe she'd remember something about him.'

Sophie found all eyes turned on her.

26

'Do *you* know anything about him, Sophie?' asked the policeman.

Sophie hesitated. What could she say? Nothing. So she shook her head, hardly daring to meet their eyes.

'Are you sure?' Lauren sounded puzzled. 'Only I thought you said he used to be married to your aunt ... ?'

There was a dead silence. Sophie was sure everyone could hear her heart pounding. She wished Ashton were here to hold her hand.

'Is this true?' The older policeman put down his pen and looked at her. 'Why didn't you mention it before? We should talk to your aunt at once.'

Sophie swallowed. 'Yes, it's true. But ... I'm afraid you won't get anything out of Aunt Angelica.'

Sophie, her parents and the police officers stood in the sitting room of Sophie's parents' cottage. Angelica sat before them in her usual rocking chair. She gazed ahead of her, barely blinking, a steady, gentle smile on her face.

'I see what you mean,' said the older policeman, staring at Angelica's vacant face.

Sophie couldn't help wishing her aunt would speak or move. But she knew she wouldn't. She had been this way since Sophie had had to demagick her.

'She doesn't respond or react to anything.' Sophie's father stroked his sister's hand gently. 'She's in a kind of coma.'

The policewoman's face was full of pity. 'I'm sorry we bothered you.' She looked around at her colleagues. 'Perhaps we should go—'

'Not so fast, not so fast . . .' The younger policeman stepped forward. 'Mrs, er – Angelica? Can you hear me?'

Angelica didn't speak. But the rocking chair creaked and Sophie realised she was rocking back and forth.

'Well, that's a start,' the policeman said cheerfully. 'Can you tell us anything about your husband? About Robert Lloyd?'

There was a long silence. Then Angelica began humming. The thin, haunting noise filled the room.

Sophie, her parents and the police officers all stood in breathless silence until the policewoman spoke.

'It's the wedding march,' she said in amazement. 'She must be remembering her wedding.' She leaned forward. 'Angelica, you're right. It's your husband we need to know about. Can you tell us anything about him?'

Angelica said nothing, just continued to hum away to herself.

'Can you think where he might go, if he was trying to hide from the world?'

Angelica went silent. Then the tune she was humming changed. It took Sophie only a few seconds to recognise it.

'"The Grand Old Duke of York". What do nursery rhymes have to do with anything?' Sophie asked her dad.

'This is getting us nowhere.' The older policeman shut his notebook with a snap. 'This poor lady is not able to communicate.' He turned to Sophie's dad. 'Thank you for your time.' He started towards the door.

Sophie didn't know what to think. Was the humming some sort of clue, or just the ramblings of a woman whose mind had been driven away?

'That's it? You're going?' Sophie's mum looked worried.

'We've done all we can here. But rest assured that there are alerts out everywhere for the Gibson children – and their parents.'

'Their parents?' Sophie felt scared.

'Of course,' he said. 'We haven't yet been able to contact them. If they turn up here or get in touch with you, please tell them to call us.'

Sophie exchanged a glance with her father. His grim expression gave nothing away.

Sophie closed the door after the police officers, but before it shut completely she saw the older policeman turn around and give their cottage a very suspicious glance.

As soon as the police car left Sophie opened the back door and let Gally – her squirrel familiar – in, shaking his ears from the cold. Rosdet – her father's fox – came more slowly. Sophie followed the familiars into the sitting room. Her mother and father were sitting on the sofa in gloomy silence. Aunt Angelica still stared into space. She had stopped humming.

Sophie's mum broke the silence. 'I wonder if Angelica does know something. Isn't there any way to get through to her, at least for a little while?' she asked.

Sophie's heart leapt. 'Yes! Of course there is! We cast a spell from *Magic Most Dark* to remagick Granny. It only lasts until midnight, but that would be enough ...' Her voice trailed off. 'Except we don't have the spell book. I dropped it into the sea after Angelica tried to use it against us. Oh!' She put her hands to her head, remembering what had gone into the spell. 'And all the ingredients are witch hunter ones.' She recalled how she'd had to break into Mr Gibson's study with Katy to get them. 'If only there was another way ...'

'There is,' said Sophie's dad, in barely a whisper. He was sitting in the shadows, his chin resting on his hand, a grim, thoughtful expression on his face. Now he looked up to meet their hopeful gazes. 'But we won't be taking it.'

'Why not?' Sophie's voice squeaked. 'It doesn't matter how difficult it is. If it gets us even one step closer to finding Ashton and Katy—'

'Because the other way would be to remagick Angelica permanently.'

Sophie's jaw dropped. 'What? You mean we can do that?' She glanced up at Angelica. 'But why haven't we done it already?'

Her father sighed. 'Because the only way to remagick a witch is to demagick another witch – to take their powers and use them to remagick Angelica. It's a witch hunter ritual, and a very cruel one. The witch we demagicked would be driven as mad as my poor sister. They could even die.'

Sophie was silent. Her father was right. She remembered vividly the terrible moment she'd had to demagick her aunt. No, she could never, ever inflict that on another innocent witch, not even to save her best friend and her boyfriend. A grey, sick misery seemed to fill her like fog. It seemed as if there was absolutely nothing they could do.

*

Sophie glanced at the clock as she laid out the plates for dinner. It was six and they still hadn't heard anything from the police. None of them were hungry, but Mum said they still had to eat something.

Her phone beeped, breaking her concentration. Sophie put down the pile of plates and got out her phone, expecting it to be Callum. But the name she read wasn't his at all.

Ashton

'Mum!' she screamed. 'Dad!'

She turned round and ran from the room. She collided with her parents in the hall.

'Ashton just texted me – just this moment!' Sophie was breathless with excitement and happiness. Her mum and dad looked on expectantly as she thumbed the text open, her hands shaking.

'He says . . .' Her eyes ran over the words. At first they didn't seem to make sense. And then, horribly, they did.

JUST TO LET YOU KNOW, UNCLE ROBERT WAS RIGHT ABOUT WITCHES LIKE YOU. YOU SHOULD ALL BE EXTERMINATED. I DIDN'T LIKE YOU ANYWAY. I WAS JUST USING YOU.

THOUGHT YOU'D LIKE TO KNOW BECAUSE I HOPE WE'LL NEVER SEE EACH OTHER AGAIN.

Sophie felt a lump in her throat, like she was trying to swallow the message but it was stuck. Her face felt hot and red and her ears were ringing as if she had been slapped hard across the face.

'What does it say?' Her father reached out and took the phone from her. He scanned the message, then wordlessly handed it to his wife and put his arms around Sophie. He pulled her into a hug. Sophie leaned against him. This couldn't be really happening. But there it was, right there on the screen.

Sophie's mum's expression turned from joy to horror as she read the text. 'Oh, Sophie,' she said gently. 'I'm sorry.' She hesitated. 'I'm so sorry, but we have to tell the police about this.'

Sophie heard her but she didn't answer. She felt numb. She closed her eyes and buried her face in her father's warm side. Her mother dialled the police and Sophie heard her speaking.

'Hello ... It's Mrs Morrow from Turlingham

Academy. Ashton Gibson has sent my daughter a text. It says . . . ' Her voice trembled as she read it out. Sophie couldn't bear to hear it again and tried to block her words out. 'Yes. Yes. No, I think "witches" is slang. You know kids, they have all kinds of words for each other.'

Sophie didn't think the 'witches' comment would do any harm. But even if it did, right now she couldn't care. Ashton hated her. He was using her. He had never liked her. Sophie felt so stupid.

'Yes. Thank you. Goodbye.' Her mum finished the call then placed the phone on the table. 'They say they may be able to trace the children's location from the text message.'

Sophie couldn't hold the tears back a second longer. She gulped and burst into sobs. Her mother hurried to join her father in hugging her.

'I c-can't believe it!' Sophie sobbed. She knew why people talked about their hearts breaking now. It felt as if her own was being wrenched in two. 'He was just using me! I don't understand! I don't understand!'

Sophie's parents hugged her tightly. Her mum kissed her head while her dad stroked her hair. Sophie sobbed and wiped her nose on her hand. She felt exhausted.

'I don't know why I fell for his stories,' she said miserably.

'Sophie, you mustn't blame yourself,' her dad said.

Her mum bent down to look into her face. 'It's not your fault. You've done nothing wrong.'

It didn't feel like that to Sophie. She started scanning her brain for something he said that could have let her know his feelings weren't genuine. All she could see was Ashton's face and it made her cry harder.

'Hey hey hey,' her mum soothed. 'How about having your friends over tonight? Erin and that lot are all still here till tomorrow morning, aren't they?' She pushed Sophie back by her shoulders. 'What a girl needs in this situation is her friends!'

Sophie managed to smile back. 'Thanks, Mum,' she said. 'That's *just* what I need.' Her mouth tipped down again, as she remembered the horrible words. 'I just wish I understood what was going on.'

As she spoke, her phone rang and vibrated on the

table. Sophie ran to pick it up, hating herself for hoping it was Ashton. It wasn't. It was Callum.

'Oh, Callum,' she began before he could speak. 'I got a text from Ashton.' Her voice wobbled. 'It didn't say where they were . . . only that he *hated* me!'

'No way. I was just ringing to tell you I'd got one from Katy. It said pretty much the same thing.'

Sophie's last shred of hope blew away. Katy and Ashton hadn't been kidnapped. They'd run away – and they must have made the enchanted letter themselves.

They were safe, and that was great. But they'd made complete fools of her and Callum. And Sophie's heart was completely broken.

THREE

Twenty minutes later, Callum was sitting with Sophie on the couch in the front room. Sophie looked at their phones, lying together on the coffee table. The police had said they would come round as soon as possible to pick the mobiles up and take them away. Sophie was glad. She felt as if she would never be able to use her phone again without thinking of Ashton's horrible message.

'What did Katy say?' she asked Callum gently. He'd hardly spoken since he got there. She felt so sorry for him. He and Katy had seemed perfect for each other.

Callum reached out and picked up his phone. He showed Sophie the message.

HI, CALLUM. I THOUGHT I SHOULD LET YOU KNOW THAT WE WENT WITH UNCLE ROBERT BECAUSE HE'S RIGHT ABOUT WITCHES. YOU SHOULD STOP BEING FRIENDS WITH THEM TOO IF YOU KNOW WHAT'S GOOD FOR YOU. JUST SO YOU KNOW, I NEVER LIKED YOU. ELFIN WARRIORS IS STUPID, AND SULPHE IS AN IDIOT. YOU ARE A JOKE.

'Oh, Callum!' Sophie exclaimed. She felt more hurt and angry than ever. How could Katy have said something so nasty?

To her surprise, Callum didn't look upset. Or at least, not as upset as he ought to.

'How can you not mind? You really like Katy!'

'Yeah, I do,' Callum answered at once. 'And Katy really likes me.'

Sophie sniffed back a tear. 'I thought Ashton liked me too ... but I guess we were wrong.'

'You shouldn't be so quick to lose faith in Ashton.

I'm not losing faith in Katy.' Callum put his phone down on the table again. 'I know Katy likes me. I know she does. I don't know why,' he shrugged, 'I'm a geek, and I'm not good-looking like Mark. I spend all my time obsessing over Elfin Warriors. But for whatever reason, she does like me.'

He sounded absolutely certain. Sophie couldn't help being impressed.

'Then why did she send that horrible message?' she objected.

'To let me know she was alive. Or to stop me from following her. Or maybe Robert Lloyd made her do it.'

Sophie was silent. It was a possibility . . .

'But how do you *know*?'

Callum turned to her, his eyes bright and hard. Sophie could tell he'd been working it over in his mind. 'The main character in Elfin Warriors isn't called Sulphe,' he said. 'She's called Serrulph.'

Sophie had had to listen to Callum talk for hours about Elfin Warriors. She knew the main character was called something like that. 'But there are loads of silly names in that game, can you seriously blame her for getting one wrong?' She rolled her eyes.

Callum laughed. 'No way! She's as big an Elfin Warriors fan as I am. Serrulph is Katy's favourite character, she wouldn't forget her name. She even dressed up as her for the fancy dress parade.'

Sophie remembered that. It did seem unlikely that Katy would forget.

'I bet that message from Ashton is the same thing. He's just trying to let you know he's alive.'

Sophie shook her head. She so much wanted it to be true, but ... She sighed. 'Well, maybe you're right. But you were going out with Katy for ages. Me and Ashton had only been together a week ...' She trailed off miserably. And there was no hiding from the fact that Ashton used to hate witches. She really hoped he hadn't meant what he said in the message, but how could she be sure? It was almost better to go on believing he hated her, than to get up her hopes again and then be disappointed.

The door opened and her mother and father walked in. With them was a plump, cheerful-looking policeman with loads of gold stripes decorating his shoulders. He had a big, toothy smile, under a moustache as brown and bristly as their kitchen broom.

'Evening all,' he said. Sophie exchanged a glance with Callum. *Did policemen really say that?*

'This is Chief Inspector Hudges,' Sophie's mother said. 'Chief Inspector, this is my daughter – Sophie – and Callum Pearce, the headmaster's son.'

'Hello,' said Sophie politely.

'Hello to you too, young lady.' Chief Inspector Hudges reached out for the phones. 'May I?'

He didn't wait for permission before opening the phones and reading both text messages. Sophie felt embarrassed to have a stranger reading Ashton's words. The man's smile widened as he read.

'Very nice,' he said. 'Yes, we'll be able to trace them now, I'm sure.' He chuckled to himself as he put the phones into a plastic bag. 'As I thought, they've simply run away. They must have talked their uncle into picking them up.' He rolled his eyes. 'Kids, eh!'

Sophie's parents didn't smile, and Sophie didn't feel much like laughing either. Even if Katy and Ashton had run away, it didn't seem right to joke about it when they weren't safely home yet.

Callum cleared his throat. His cheeks were a little red but he sounded calm as he said, 'You can't be sure they've run away.'

'We've seen this kind of thing a thousand times before. We professionals know a little more about these cases than you do,' Chief Inspector Hudges said with another of his toothy smiles.

'You don't know more about *Katy* than I do!' Sophie could tell Callum was angry. 'I'm her boyfriend and I'm sure she would never run away.'

Hudges' smile drooped slightly. 'You're sure, are you? Been going out long?'

'Yes. Since the end of the half-term holidays . . .' His voice tailed off, and Sophie knew they were thinking the same thing . . . that wasn't really all that long.

'Suppose that does seem a long time when you're a kid,' Hudges said, smirking to Sophie's mum, who didn't smile back. Sophie wanted to tell him off for being so patronising, but she didn't think it would help.

'Well, Mrs Morrow,' he continued, 'you might like to know we've been looking for reasons Katy might have run away. We've been talking to her ex-boyfriend to see if she's made contact.'

Sophie and Callum glanced at each other. *Ex-boyfriend?* Sophie couldn't believe that Katy hadn't mentioned him before.

'Didn't know about him, eh?' Hudges sounded triumphant as he looked at Callum. 'Don't know quite as much about Katy as you thought, eh? His name's Tristan Blackwood. They were very keen on each other. In fact, we think Katy might try to visit him. We're investigating.'

Callum clenched his fists. 'I don't care what you think. And I don't care who Katy used to go out with. She's with me now.'

Sophie wished she could speak out to back him up. But how could she be sure Callum was right? Hudges didn't have any reason to lie, after all.

He knelt down beside Katy and Callum. 'Look, kids, I know you're worried. And hurting. But it's most likely that Katy is with her uncle, and that she wants to see her old boyfriend. Isn't that better than them being kidnapped?'

'You don't know,' said Callum. 'If you had seen the other texts she's sent me—'

Hudges narrowed his eyes. 'Most teenage girls sign their texts with kisses, you know. So I wouldn't go thinking an xx makes you special.'

Sophie listened to his heavy tread going towards the door, and the muffled sound of voices as he said goodbye to her parents. Callum was sitting with his head in his hands. She wished she could do something, say something, to make things better – but she just didn't know what to think any more. It seemed as if Ashton and Katy had run away from school. They had run away from her.

FOUR

Sophie hugged the duvet around her knees as she sat up in bed. All her friends – Erin, Joanna, Kaz and Lauren – had come round and they were getting comfy on the floor in their sleeping bags and blankets. Lauren was doing Joanna's hair, Kaz and Erin were watching a music video on Erin's phone and joking about the hot lead singer. Sophie's mum had let them have cookies as long as Sophie cleared up all the crumbs the next morning. But there was one person missing, and Sophie knew none of them could forget it.

'I just can't believe Katy would run away with her

uncle,' said Lauren, for what seemed like the hundredth time.

'I know.' Erin looked up at once. 'If only she'd told us how she was feeling, maybe we could have helped.'

'But what happened to her parents?' Kaz puzzled. 'Why didn't they show up to collect them? Hey,' she grinned, 'do you remember when they first arrived, and they came in a limousine? We all thought Ashton looked just like Jareth Quinn.' Her smile faded. 'Sorry, Sophie. I shouldn't have reminded you.'

Sophie was about to reply when she heard a scratching at the window next to her. She kneeled up on her bed, and drew the curtains apart. Gally was perching on the windowsill, his bushy tail up like an umbrella, his bright, intelligent eyes watching her.

'A squirrel! A *black* squirrel!' Lauren cried out behind her. 'That's so cute!'

'Oh um, yeah.' Sophie tried to laugh as her friends crowded on to the bed with her, clamouring to see the squirrel. 'I've been feeding him for ages. He waits on my windowsill for scraps.' She opened the window and gave Gally a biscuit.

'He's so tame,' Erin said in astonishment.

'Will he eat a bit of biscuit from me?' Lauren held her cookie out to him. Gally took it and nibbled it. The girls squealed and laughed.

'Too cute,' Erin giggled.

'I better close the window,' said Sophie, throwing Gally a look to apologise for shutting him out. 'It's cold out there,' she added.

The girls' laughter died away.

'I hope Katy and Ashton are somewhere warm,' said Lauren.

'I hope they're not . . . not in danger.' Joanna's voice was very small. 'I wish there was some way we could find out.'

'We could always ask the Forces of the Earth,' said Erin with a nervous giggle.

Sophie's breath caught in her chest. Had one of her friends guessed the truth about her? 'You know, like when we did that séance up in the lighthouse, ages ago, before Katy even arrived . . . '

Back when I was just pretending *to do magic!* Sophie thought. *Phew . . .*

But Erin's words had also given her an idea. She was annoyed with herself for not thinking of it before. 'That's an amazing idea!' Sophie exclaimed, jumping to her feet. 'I've got some candles here.' She ran across the room and pulled open her drawer, rummaging through it to find lemon-scented ones and incense. She turned back to her friends. 'Lauren, draw the curtains. Jo, turn the light off.' Her friends jumped into action. 'Everyone get in a circle. We're going to ask the Forces of the Earth to help us find Katy and Ashton.'

'Great idea!' Erin agreed. 'Hey, it's quarter to midnight. Let's start the séance at the exact stroke of twelve – then it'll be even more likely to work, right?'

'Erin, it's not real!' Kaz laughed and rolled her eyes. 'But it does sound like it'd help – you know, if it *was* real.'

The girls got into a circle, giggling nervously. Sophie settled down with them and lit three candles. In the darkened room they glowed like a star.

Sophie reached out her hands to Erin on one side and Lauren on the other.

'Now think about Katy and Ashton,' she told them.

'Imagine them as you last saw them. Imagine them as if they were standing right in front of you.'

The girls waited silently, except for the odd muffled giggle and whisper. Sophie watched the lit numbers on the dial of her alarm clock count down to twelve. She concentrated on imagining Ashton's face, floating in front of her. His deep green eyes and his long dark eyelashes ... The way he smiled at her ... Her heart beat faster. And as the numbers turned to zeroes, she said softly:

'Repeat after me ... Forces of the Earth.'

'Forces of the Earth,' chorused the girls.

Sophie felt her Source tingle, the familiar magic flowing through her fingertips and her whole body. She couldn't help smiling. She never got tired of this feeling. It was as if she'd been plugged into an electric circuit. The whole world felt brighter, sparkling and glittering with a fierce, wild power.

'Earth, water, wind and fire.'

'Earth, water, wind and fire.'

'Use your great powers to show us the people we want to see.'

At once, the room filled with a spicy, rich scent. Sophie could hear the others sniffing.

'It smells like woodsmoke . . . or incense . . .' Lauren said in a small, awed voice. 'Where's it coming from?'

'The candles,' Kaz said, then added, 'Of course.' But she didn't sound so sure.

'Are you kidding me?' Erin exclaimed. 'It's Dark Stranger for Men.'

'Ashton's aftershave!' Sophie cried. A rush of emotion flooded over her. It felt as if Ashton was right back in the room with her, hugging her and laughing with her. Except none of those things had meant anything. She swallowed, suddenly wanting to cry.

'That's scary,' Lauren's voice wobbled.

'It's magic! This is so cool!' Erin sat up. 'And hey – I can see something in the candle flame.'

Sophie leaned forward. The wax had melted and dribbled down the side of the candle to form a five-petalled shape.

'It looks just like a daisy,' she said. She felt herself shudder. 'Katy's favourite earrings are shaped like daisies!' Sophie had given them to her. They were gold and she had put them in her friendship bracelet to protect her from witches … it didn't work against witch hunters though.

'Oh, you're just seeing what you want to see.' Kaz sat back. 'That could be anything. Right, Joanna?'

Joanna giggled nervously.

'It doesn't mean anything,' Kaz grumbled.

'I think it means they're safe,' said Sophie softly. 'Wherever they are, I think they're OK.' She wasn't sure how she knew, she just sensed it.

'Yeah, of course they are,' Erin joined in. The others agreed. Sophie knew they were trying to reassure each other, but it didn't matter. She was sure the spell had worked – and then she heard something: a scream.

And it was Katy who was screaming.

It seemed to come through the wall, echoing in the chimney. Sophie whirled round, but the muffled scream faded as quickly as it had arrived. The other girls squealed in fear, and Lauren gripped Sophie's hand so tightly that her nails bit in.

'What was *that*?' Even Kaz sounded shaken.

'It was a scream!' Erin gasped.

'It was *Katy's* scream,' Joanna said in a terrified voice.

'Sophie, I don't like this. Let's turn on the lights.' Lauren was almost sobbing.

'Calm down!' Kaz had got her composure back. 'Sophie's parents are watching TV downstairs. It was probably just a noise from the film. Right, Sophie?'

Sophie hesitated. She was sure it was Katy's voice – she would have known it anywhere. But there was no point in scaring her friends. She'd have to work out what to do about this tomorrow. For now, at least she knew that Katy and Ashton were alive.

But if that really was Katy screaming, then how long would they be alive for?

The courtyard in front of Turlingham Academy was emptying fast, as cars and buses arrived to take the last students home for the holidays. Sophie hugged herself, not just against the cold, as she watched parents greeting their sons and daughters, and heard the happy laughter of her classmates preparing to go home for the holidays. Where were Ashton and Katy now, she wondered. And where were their parents?

She smiled as Joanna came running up to her, her cheeks pink in the chilly air.

'Bye, Sophie. I'll see you next term.'

'Have a great holiday!' Sophie hugged her.

Joanna held her shoulders and looked her in the eyes.

'You promise you'll text if you hear anything?'

All her friends had said the same thing before they left.

'I promise.'

Callum came up to them, wrapped up in a scarf and hat. He looked tired but he managed a smile for Joanna.

'Have a great holiday, Callum.' Joanna waved as she walked away towards her parents' red hatchback car.

'How are you doing?' Sophie looked at Callum with concern.

'I couldn't sleep last night.'

Sophie put a comforting hand on his arm. 'Let's go and get a hot chocolate at mine.'

They walked along the winding path through the pine trees, back towards Sophie's cottage. There were patches of ice in the mud and Sophie had to be careful not to slip. As she drew near to her home, Gally bounded out of the trees and twirled around her legs, almost tripping her up.

'Careful, Gally!' Sophie reached down to pick him up, but he dodged her and ran back into the trees, looking back as if he wanted her to follow.

Sophie and Callum went after him. Gally jumped up on to a tree stump. There was a gap in the trees through which Sophie could see her cottage. A police car was parked in front of it, and Sophie's mum was just shutting the front door after a policeman who was leaving the house and walking down the drive to the car.

'It's that Chief Inspector guy,' said Callum. He didn't sound pleased. 'Hudges, or whatever his name is.'

Hudges opened the car door, got in and drove away.

'Let's go and see what's happened.' Sophie made to

run back down the slope, but Callum caught her arm to slow her down.

'I don't trust him.' His face was serious as they walked to the cottage. 'I was thinking about this last night. He hadn't seen any of Katy's old texts, only the one from yesterday.'

'So what?' Sophie said, feeling desperate to get back to the house.

'Well, he said that thing about Katy signing off her texts with two kisses.'

Sophie started to pay attention. He *had* said that hadn't he? Sophie remembered thinking it was rude and patronising.

'How would he have known?' asked Callum.

Sophie thought about it. It was weird. 'What do you think is going on?' she asked. 'That the police know more than they are saying?'

'I don't know ... I just ... I don't trust him,' he added.

Sophie, pushing open the gate, didn't answer at once. Callum was right, it was suspicious. But then, Katy's text had been so horrible. Maybe Callum was just deluding himself, trying to believe that Katy and Ashton hadn't run away from them. There was a miserable weight in her stomach as she thought of it, like a big grey stone. And then she remembered the scream she had heard the night before. Katy's scream. Perhaps Callum was right. Perhaps Katy hadn't wanted to go with her uncle after all.

She opened her mouth to tell Callum about the séance, but before she could speak, the front door was whisked open. Her mother stood there, and Sophie could feel the excitement and relief blazing out of her before she even spoke.

'Sophie! Callum!' she exclaimed. 'I was just coming to find you – it's the most wonderful news!'

Sophie glanced at Callum, before her mum swept her into a joyful hug.

'They've found them!' Sophie's mum announced. 'Chief Inspector Hudges came to tell us that they've found Katy and Ashton!'

Sophie couldn't believe her ears but she felt weightless, as if she might just float away. The worry was over. Katy and Ashton were safe!

FIVE

'When did they find them?' Sophie exclaimed at the same second Callum said: 'Where?'

'Slow down, slow down.' Sophie's mum laughed, finally letting Sophie go. Her eyes were sparkling and she wore a smile as bright as a lighthouse beam as she ushered them in and shut the door. 'They found them last night, safe and well.'

'But where are they?' Sophie hopped up and down with impatience. 'Can I talk to them? What happened?'

'They're at their house in Sheffield. It turns out the

two of them decided to run away – some silly fight with their parents. One of Hudges' colleagues brought them back at about ten p.m. last night.'

'That's great!' Sophie grinned, but then felt Callum tugging her sleeve. She glanced up at him. He didn't look as happy as she'd expected him to. Then she realised what was troubling her.

'Didn't Mr and Mrs Gibson call to say they were OK?' she asked. 'They said they would.'

'They didn't, but that's no surprise, they must have had far too much on their mind to think of it.' She added, laughing, 'You'd better never do this to me, Sophie – I'd die of worry. Anyway, didn't you say they don't have a phone right now?' She turned back to the house. 'I must call the school board. They'll be so relieved . . . ' Her voice faded away as she ran back to her study.

Left on their own, Sophie turned to look at Callum. His face was serious, and he simply shook his head at her.

'There's no way they wouldn't get in touch,' he said. 'They promised.'

Sophie bit her lip. She wanted to be happy and relieved that Ashton and Katy were safe, but Callum had a point. And then her eyes widened as the most obvious problem of all struck her.

'At their house in Sheffield?' she said. 'There's no way that's true. The witch hunters are watching it. If they were with their parents they wouldn't go home.'

'Exactly.' Callum's brows furrowed.

'And then there was the scream!'

'Scream?' Callum looked worried.

Sophie explained quickly. Callum's frown deepened as she talked.

'And Mum said they were brought home at ten last night, but we did the spell at midnight – two whole hours later!'

'There's only one way to find out for sure if they're OK,' Callum said. 'We've got to go there. See for ourselves.'

Sophie's heart sped up. 'You mean go to Sheffield?'

Callum nodded.

That was a crazy idea, wasn't it? But Sophie couldn't take the chance that someone was lying and Katy and

Ashton weren't safe. Callum was right, they had to see for themselves.

'The only thing is ... how do we get to Sheffield?' Callum muttered. 'I don't suppose your mum would take us?'

'No – at least not today. You heard her, she totally believes the police's story.'

'Well, we've got to get there quickly. If Hudges is lying to your mum ... ' Callum trailed off.

'Then Katy and Ashton could be in even worse trouble than we thought,' Sophie said. There was a pause as they both stood there, racking their brains for a way to get to Sheffield. Then Sophie turned around and looked towards the door. 'Joanna!' she exclaimed. 'She lives in Durham. Her family could drop us off in Sheffield on the way.'

Sophie grabbed her coat, flung open the door and together they ran back up the path to the courtyard. Sophie's mum would kill her for running off like this, but it was an emergency. She scanned the courtyard. She spotted the red hatchback – Joanna was just getting into the back seat.

'Hey, Jo! Wait!' Sophie and Callum ran over to the car, yelling and waving. Joanna's mother poked her head out of the driver's seat, and Joanna looked up, surprised.

Sophie reached them, out of breath.

'They've found Katy and Ashton! They're safe ... they're home ... ' she told them.

'That's great!' Joanna shouted and gave Sophie a hug.

'We have to see them, we need a lift. Please?' Callum said.

'A *lift*? To Sheffield?' Joanna looked doubtful.

'Yes please,' said Sophie. 'Would that be all right, Mrs Grey?'

Joanna's mum ran a hand through her hair and sighed. 'As long as it's OK with your parents.'

Sophie hesitated. There was no way her mum would let her go haring off to Sheffield on no notice, and there was no time to persuade her.

'What now?' whispered Callum.

Then she remembered ... if Robert had managed it, she could too!

'Wait right there,' she told them all. 'Please!'

She turned round and raced off, back to her own house. She let herself in with her latch key. Her mother was on the phone in the study. Sophie didn't have any trouble in getting up to her own room without being seen, the only thing that got in her way was the guilt. But some things were more important.

Once in her room, she ripped a piece of paper out of her notebook and scribbled a few words on it.

Dear Mrs Grey,

It's fine for Sophie and Callum to go to Sheffield with you.

All the best, Mrs Morrow and Mr Pearce

It wouldn't fool anyone . . . yet.

Sophie looked around her room for inspiration. On her windowsill was her collection of plants that she had watered that morning. She picked up her spider plant and tipped some of the moist soil on to the paper.

'Earth, water, air and fire,' she murmured, rubbing the soil on to the paper with her fingertips. 'Let this message take root and grow in the reader's mind!'

She folded the note up and put it in her pocket. Then she grabbed her school bag and quickly flung in some clothes. Gally made her jump, bounding off the wardrobe and scampering in along with them.

'Of course I wouldn't forget you!' she told him. She zipped up the bag, leaving a little hole for Gally to breathe through.

She went down the stairs quickly and quietly. Her mum was still in the study on the phone, and her dad was nowhere to be seen. Sophie slipped out of the front door and raced back to Joanna's car.

'Here you are,' she gasped, handing the note to Joanna's mum. 'Both our parents said it was fine.'

'I don't know, Sophie ...' Joanna's mum looked doubtful as she took the letter and opened it. Sophie watched her eyes move across the paper. In a couple of seconds, a vague, pleasant smile had replaced her doubtful expression.

'Oh, well that explains it all,' she said, folding up the note and putting it into the glove compartment. 'What are you waiting for? Hop in!'

'Yay!' Joanna punched the air. 'Road trip!'

Sophie went round to get in the other passenger side. She couldn't help grinning at Callum's amazed expression.

'Nice one,' Callum whispered to her as they got into the car. 'Can you do me a sick note for rugby?'

Sophie smiled. Inside, she wasn't feeling so great. She knew her parents would be frantic when they realised she was gone ...

As they were driving out of the village of Turlingham, the guilt got too much for Sophie and she fumbled in her pocket for her phone, to send her mum a text, just to let her know that they were OK and they'd be back as soon as they could. But she found her pocket empty. Of course – Hudges had taken both of their phones!

I'm so sorry, Mum ...

But there was no turning back now. She needed to get to the bottom of this mystery about Ashton and Katy. She would just have to deal with the consequences later.

SIX

Mrs Grey pulled up in front of the Gibsons' house and Sophie got out of the car.

Was anyone inside? She scanned the huge, half-timbered house, but the leaded windows and the thick net curtains made it impossible to tell.

'Are you sure this is the one?' Joanna's mother sounded worried. 'It doesn't look as if anyone's home – there's no car in the drive.'

'Oh yes, I'm sure they're home.' Sophie hurriedly picked up her bag. Callum followed. Sophie wasn't at all sure, but she didn't need Joanna's mum getting suspicious. 'They always put their car in the garage.'

'See you next term, Sophie!' Joanna yelled. 'Say hi to Katy for me.' Joanna waved and Sophie waved back, doing her best to hide her nerves. She waited for Joanna's mother to drive on, but she didn't move.

'Er – goodbye,' Sophie said again. 'And thanks for the lift!' She turned and began walking up the path between the dark fir trees, hoping that Joanna's mum would take the hint and drive off. She glanced around when she didn't hear the engine start. Joanna's mum smiled at her encouragingly.

'You must be in a hurry. There's no need to wait around for us,' Callum said hopefully as he followed Sophie.

Joanna's mum checked her watch. 'I'll wait till you're safely inside.'

Sophie and Callum exchanged a worried glance. There was nothing to do but walk on up the path towards the front door, and hope that the Gibsons answered – or that Joanna's mum would get bored and drive off. Sophie looked up at the ivy-covered porch. The strands danced in the breeze.

'It doesn't look as if they're home,' Callum whispered. 'What are we going to do?'

Sophie swallowed as they stepped into the shadow of the porch. She put her thumb on the bell and pressed it firmly. Inside the house, she could hear distant chimes.

'I'll think of something,' she whispered back.

The next moments felt like hours to Sophie. She listened, using all her witch powers, hoping to hear someone coming down the stairs or out of a room to answer the door. There was no sound. The house was silent – and then Sophie noticed that the post was still in the letterbox, halfway in and halfway out. It looked as if the Gibsons really weren't there. She nudged Callum and pointed it out. Callum grimaced.

Sophie turned and looked to where Joanna's mum was still waiting. Joanna's mum waved and smiled, but didn't start the engine. Sophie managed a smile in return, then turned back to the door. What were they going to do?

'We can't stand here all night,' Callum whispered.

Sophie made up her mind. It was dangerous to do magic in front of Joanna and her mum, but hopefully they were far enough away that they wouldn't notice.

She took a strand of ivy and rubbed it between her fingers, feeling the familiar tingle in her Source. The crescent-moon ring glowed.

'Forces of the Earth,' she murmured, 'make this ivy grow as fast as the wind!'

The ivy began putting out new shoots at once. Sophie guided them towards the lock. She held her breath as the ivy crept into the lock and into the crack between the door and the frame. The wood creaked and groaned – and then with a click the door jumped open. It worked!

Sophie pushed the door open, and hurried in. She could see at once that the house was dark and cold. There was no one there.

'Hello, Katy! Hi, Ashton!' she said as loudly as she could. Callum crowded in behind her, using his taller build to block Joanna's mum's view. Sophie went into the hall and Callum turned, waving. 'Bye! Bye, Joanna! See you next term!'

Sophie blew out her cheeks with relief as she heard the engine start and the car drive away. Callum shut the door and leaned his back against it. He grinned at her.

Sophie let Gally out of her bag. He jumped on to the floor, his nose twitching as he sniffed around the hall.

'Nice acting, Sophie!' Callum said. Then the smile faded from his face. Sophie realised he was looking over her shoulder. She turned around quickly, and saw what she hadn't noticed before. The door at the end of the hall had been kicked in. The wood was splintered.

Sophie gasped.

'Looks like someone got here before us,' Callum said grimly. He stepped forward, his feet crunching on broken glass.

'Careful of the glass, Gally!' Sophie warned, and Gally hopped around it. 'What if that someone's still here?' she whispered to Callum.

There was a terrified silence. Sophie was sure she could hear her own heart pounding. Robert could be anywhere in this dark, silent house. There could be witch hunters everywhere. It could be a trap!

'This place is empty,' said Callum slowly. He was looking at the kicked-in door. 'And here's how I know.' He reached out and brushed his fingers across the doorway. Sophie looked at the thick, dusty cobweb he showed her. 'This break-in happened ages ago, long enough ago for a spider to have spun a web across the doorway.'

'Callum, you're a genius.' Sophie clapped him on the shoulder, terror turning to relief.

Callum smiled and blushed and shrugged. 'We don't always have to rely on magic.'

Sophie, Callum and Gally made their way through the house. Every room was wrecked; drawers were pulled open and clothes strewn everywhere, mirrors shattered, windows cracked and furniture splintered. Even the garage was ransacked: hedge clippers lying open on the ground, bikes pulled down from their stands and tipped over on the floor. Last of all, Callum opened the hatch to the attic, climbed up and shone a torch around cautiously.

'No one,' he reported, jumping back down the last few rungs of the ladder. 'The Gibsons aren't here, and I bet they haven't been for a while.'

'So Hudges was lying.' Sophie frowned. 'But why? I don't get it. Is he involved, somehow? Is that why Mr and Mrs Gibson were so scared of the police?'

'We'd better look for clues,' Callum said, switching off the torch. 'You start up here. I'll look downstairs.'

Sophie went straight to Katy's room. *Come on, Katy, give me a clue*, she thought as she pushed open the door.

She and Gally searched through piles of clothes and sifted through papers. There was nothing that seemed like a clue, just recipes for witch hunter spells and old homework books. Sophie picked up a photo album that had been thrown face-down on the bed. A photo slipped out and floated to the floor. Gally ran over, picked it up and handed it to her.

The first thing she saw was Katy, smiling and happy. The second thing she saw was that Katy had her arm around a boy's shoulders. And the boy wasn't Callum.

At a glance she could see that the boy was handsome. He had piercing blue eyes and curly dark blond hair, and an air of subtle confidence. The kind of boy who would be captain of the rugby team and head of the school.

She turned the photo over. On the back, in firm black pen, was written: *Lots of love, Tris xx.*

Tris? Sophie's heart felt as if it were sinking into the floor. Hadn't Hudges said that Katy had an ex called Tristan? Tristan Black or something? She looked at the photo again. Suddenly it didn't look as if they were just friends.

'Find anything?'

Sophie jumped, and automatically put the photo behind her back. Callum walked into the room.

'This isn't a burglary,' he announced. 'They've left the TV, the computer, the iPad. I even found a safe in Mr and Mrs Gibson's room. It had been opened but all the jewellery was still there. This has got to be witch hunters.'

Sophie nodded wordlessly.

Callum's gaze dropped to her hand. 'Why have you got your hands behind your back?' he asked.

'I ... um ...' Sophie didn't want to show him the photo. It would only upset him. But Callum held out his hand.

'Come on, Sophie.'

Sophie reluctantly passed him the photo. She could hardly bear to look at Callum's face as he studied it and then turned it over to read the message on the back.

'It ... it looks as if Hudges was telling the truth that time,' she said quietly. 'Maybe Katy and Ashton have gone on the run with their parents. Maybe Hudges just couldn't tell us the truth because—'

'No!'

She jumped. Callum's eyes were angry and a frown creased his forehead.

'I don't believe it. Hudges is a liar, I can tell. I bet you anything he's a witch hunter himself.' He strode up and down the room. 'If only there was a way to find out.' He stopped and frowned at the photo again.

'There *is* a way to find out!' Sophie exclaimed. How could she have forgotten? 'The witch hunter family

74

trees. Mr Gibson keeps them in his study. If Hudges is a witch hunter, his name will be on it.' *And if it isn't,* she thought as they ran downstairs, *we've just got to hope that Katy and Ashton are safe with their parents somewhere.*

In the study, Sophie went straight to the shelves of huge, leather-bound books.

'These weigh a ton!' Callum panted as he helped her heave them on to the table in a plume of dust.

'Yeah. It's not just the Gibson family tree in here – the witch hunters only marry witch hunters so they keep a record of all the other family trees too. Ashton told me.' Sophie opened one of the books and let the thick, creamy pages flop open. Each page showed a branch of a family tree, the names written out in flowing fountain pen.

'This is going to take for ever,' Callum groaned, and began reading. Sophie did too, scanning up and down the index for the name Hudges. Gibson, Drakenfield, Furlong, Voss . . . name after name that wasn't Hudges. Sophie read until her head spun with a kaleidoscope of witch hunters.

'Nothing,' she said finally, shutting the last book. She looked at Callum, who was just coming to the end of his last volume too. 'Hudges isn't a witch hunter. Now do you believe me?'

'No!' Callum's angry exclamation made Sophie jump. 'I don't. There's got to be more evidence.'

Sophie looked back at the page in front of her, sighing. Callum was clearly in denial. His girlfriend had run off, and he wouldn't believe it. How was she going to convince him? Then she spotted a name she recognised.

Blackwood. Now she remembered – *Tristan Blackwood*. That was Katy's ex-boyfriend's name.

On a whim, she turned to the page. The first name, Llewellyn Blackwood, had died in 1134.

'Look at this, Callum,' she said, pointing to the page. 'The Blackwood family's ancient – it goes back centuries. It's the oldest family I've seen so far. I bet they are really powerful. And Katy went out with one of them!'

Callum grunted, not sounding impressed. Sophie winced, realising she'd been a bit insensitive. She traced the line downwards. Right at the bottom she found what she'd expected: Tristan Blackwood, the son of Siegfried and Aurora Blackwood.

'Maybe we should try and get in touch with him,' she said thoughtfully, running her fingers over his name. 'Even if Hudges is lying about Katy going to see him, maybe he knows something that might help.' She hesitated. Under her fingertips she could feel indentations in the paper.

'I don't care about Tristan Blackwood,' Callum said crossly. 'That's all in Katy's past.'

Sophie heard him, but she was busy trying to work out what the indentations were. She pulled the desk lamp over and shone it on to the spot where she had felt them, right next to Tristan's name.

'Hey, look! Something's been rubbed out,' she said. 'Right here, where the name of Tristan's wife would go.'

Callum leaned over to look.

'Interesting . . .' He grabbed a piece of paper from the printer tray and a pencil from the desk. He put the paper over the indentations and rubbed the pencil across it, shading the paper grey. White fine marks began to appear in the grey.

'I saw this on an old TV programme ...' Callum grinned, as the white marks increased. 'Hey, cool, it's actually working! I can almost read it – it's a name – it's ...'

Sophie leaned over to see why he had gone silent. In an instant, she saw why.

The name was Katy Gibson.

'Wow. Someone was really sure Katy was going to marry Tristan Blackwood!' she gasped.

Callum pushed himself away from the desk, his face scowling and furious. He stormed out of the room, letting the door slam behind him.

Sophie realised this was how boys dealt with a broken heart.

SEVEN

'Callum,' Sophie called, as she went from room to room trying to find him. She looked in Mr and Mrs Gibsons' room, in the bathroom and in the spare bedroom. Finally, she found him. He was pacing back and forth in Katy's bedroom. Sophie's heart ached as she saw the miserable expression on his face.

'I don't understand,' he muttered. 'Why did she pretend to like me?'

Gally jumped from Sophie's shoulder on to Callum's and nuzzled into his neck.

'What do you mean, "pretend" to like you?' She shook Callum gently. 'She really does like you!'

'Yeah, right.' Callum shrugged her off, gently put Gally on the bed, and went on pacing. 'Why would she never talk about him unless she was hiding something? Why would she like me when she's got him? I mean, he's the heir to the oldest, most powerful witch hunter family in the world. I'm just a geek who likes crosswords and Elfin Warriors.'

'And you're funny, and intelligent, and . . . there are a million reasons for her to like you!' Sophie looked hopefully at Callum, but he was still hanging his head. 'I know she likes you. I can tell.'

'After that text message?' Callum gave a small, humourless laugh.

Their roles had reversed – now it was Callum's turn to have doubts. Sophie was absolutely certain that Katy liked Callum. She looked around Katy's room desperately. There had to be some way of convincing Callum he was wrong. She couldn't bear to see him looking so beaten and hopeless.

Her gaze fell on a little figure of a pointy-eared elf.

It sat on the edge of Katy's desk – just where she would have looked at it every time she sat down to use her computer.

'Look at this.' She crossed to the desk and picked up the figure. She held it out to Callum. 'You two used to play Elfin Warriors together all the time. She wouldn't have kept this figure of Sulphe if she didn't like you.'

Callum smiled reluctantly as he took it. 'I gave her this,' he said. Then he hesitated. 'Sophie, what did you just say?'

'That she wouldn't have kept it if she didn't like you.'

'No, what did you call the elf?' Sophie was startled by the excitement that crackled in Callum's voice.

'Uh … Sulphe. No wait, it's Serrulph, isn't it? Or something. Whatever. Does it matter?'

'Yes!' Callum slapped his head. 'Because Katy said Sulphe when she knows it's Serrulph. And Sulphe is an anagram!' He ran around the room until he found a pen, then quickly scribbled on the back of a piece of paper. 'Duh, why didn't I see that before? Look what happens when you rearrange the letters.'

He flipped the paper round to show her.

Help us.

There was a horrified silence. Sophie's knees felt weak and she sat down hard on the bed. Terrified thoughts raced around her head. So Katy and Ashton were a long way from safe. The message proved that they'd been kidnapped.

'What are we going to do?' she said, trembling. 'Hudges and the police aren't even looking for them any more. They think they're safe. I just don't know how ... maybe the witch hunters enchanted Hudges to make him think that?'

'Maybe,' said Callum. He clenched the figure of Serrulph in his fist. 'And maybe not. The important thing is that we're the only ones who know the truth. We've got to find them ourselves – and fast.'

'Find them, but how?' Sophie looked around the ransacked room. She answered her own question. 'Look for clues. Anything. Any kind of hint about where they might have gone.'

Together, Sophie and Callum ran to the study. Sophie pulled open desk drawers, and Callum rifled through the open safe. There were letters and files and newspaper clippings, but none of them mentioned Robert. Sophie began to panic. They had to find a way to help Katy and Ashton quickly, before Robert harmed them.

There were so many pages, and skimming through them, they all seemed to blur into one. Over and over, page after page, Sophie's eyes went up and down the paper, up and down ... She realised a simple, annoying tune was running through her head: *He marched them up to the top of the hill and he marched them down again. Oh the Grand Old Duke of York* ...

'That tune!' she said, putting down the envelope she was holding.

'What tune?' Callum looked up.

'"The Grand Old Duke of York". It's a nursery rhyme ... and the last time I heard it was when Angelica was being questioned about Robert's whereabouts. She started humming it.' Why was she thinking about it now? 'I must have seen something,' Sophie murmured. She turned back to the hill of photo albums and diaries and documents that she'd already been through. 'Come on, Callum, help me. We're looking for the Grand Old Duke of York!'

Callum dived in. Gally joined them, and for a few moments there was silence except for the rustling of paper and flapping of pages. Then Callum, who was flicking through a gigantic photo album, exclaimed: 'Oh my god, I've found it!'

Sophie dropped the letter she was reading and craned over to see what he was looking at. 'What?'

Callum's finger stabbed down on an old photograph of a pub in front of a steep, grassy hillside. A sign hanging outside the old stone building proclaimed it to be 'The Duke of York'.

'That must be it!' Sophie cried. She'd skimmed over the photo without a thought – but the name must have lodged in her mind.

Callum unpeeled the photo from the page and turned it over. In faded biro, someone had written: 'Holiday with Robert. Bordley, Yorkshire. Great Yorkshire puddings!'

Callum turned round to look at Sophie, one eyebrow raised. 'Angelica was humming that tune? Do you think it was a coincidence?'

Sophie shook her head slowly. A tingle went down her spine and her crescent-moon ring glinted. This felt like a proper clue! Angelica had been telling them where he was after all.

'Well, we can google Bordley!' He reached into his pocket and then frowned. 'Oh – Hudges has still got my phone.'

'We can use Mr Gibson's computer,' Sophie said. She went to the computer desk, switched the computer on and it hummed to life, lights winking. Callum sat down in front of the keyboard and Sophie hopped from foot to foot with impatience while the computer started up. Callum opened a browser and typed the name of the pub and the village into the search engine.

The map opened. 'It's in the middle of nowhere!' Sophie said.

'The middle of the Yorkshire Moors, to be precise.' Callum zoomed in. 'Just a few farms around. The pub should be really easy to find – there can't be more than one in that tiny village.'

'Nice one, Callum!' Sophie put up her hand for a high five and Callum slapped it. It felt as if they were finally getting somewhere.

'I'll look for the best way of getting there.' Callum hunched over the computer, his fingers dancing across the keyboard. As he did so, Sophie went to the window and peeped through the curtains. What she saw made her freeze. There was a police car at the kerb.

'OK, so Bordley doesn't have a train station,' Callum began, behind her. 'We'll have to go to Skipton—'

'Callum!' Sophie hissed, dropping the curtain.

Callum turned, startled. Sophie beckoned him over. Together they peeked around the edge of the curtain. A man was just getting out of the police car, his phone nestled between his chin and his shoulder as he reached for his bag. He turned to look up at the house.

It was Chief Inspector Hudges!

Sophie and Callum ducked down as one.

Sophie's blood was pumping. She put a finger to

her lips as Callum began to whisper to her. She concentrated hard, using her powerful witch hearing to listen in on Hudges' conversation. She could just make it out, as distant as if he were on a crackly old phone line.

'Yes, Mr Blackwood. No, sir. I'm there now. No, I put the headmistress off the scent . . .' He was talking about Sophie's mum! ' . . . but then the kids went missing so they called the station. I managed to trace a school friend who dropped them off here on their way to Durham . . .' Joanna! Sophie hoped she hadn't put her in danger too. 'No, she doesn't know a thing. Our interest is in the two children, Sophie and Callum.'

Sophie jumped as a metallic sound grated in her ear, and then she heard Hudges say 'What the . . . ?'

Hudges had put a key in the lock – and discovered her trick with the vines!

She grabbed Callum's arm and pulled him after her to the door. As silently and quickly as she could, she raced downstairs, Callum panting behind her. In the hall, she could see the front door opening. She swung left, through the kitchen door, and across the black and white tiles to the door to the garage. She unlocked it and darted through. Callum followed. Sophie turned and locked the door behind her. She could hear Hudges' boots tramping into the kitchen.

She looked around. Callum was astride a mountain bike, and was holding another one out to her. He nodded sharply at the garage door. Sophie didn't need a second more prompting. She hit the switch that opened the garage door, swung her bag across her shoulder and held it open for Gally to jump inside. The bike fitted her well – it had to be Katy's. She was already pedalling to the garage door as it swung open.

Sophie rode as fast as she could, swooping after Callum down the drive, bouncing off the kerb and speeding up the road. So Hudges was in this up to his bushy eyebrows. He was working with the witch hunters. Namely, the Blackwoods. And if the book was anything to go by, they were a very powerful family of witch hunters.

EIGHT

'There's the station!' Callum gasped as he cycled through the traffic, pointing ahead of them to a honey-coloured stone building with a glass roof and a big sign outside.

'Finally!' Sophie's chest was burning and her knees were aching from pedalling. Sheffield had a lot of hills! She followed Callum across the road, not daring to wait for the lights to change. A chorus of indignant car horns saluted them as she jumped off the bicycle and let it slide to the floor, wheels still spinning.

'Just leave them,' Callum panted, leaping off his

bicycle too. He raced into the ticket hall and Sophie followed him, dodging the startled passengers to the ticket booth. Three people were waiting and she had to hide her impatience, shifting from foot to foot until it was her turn. She had about twenty pounds on her, money she'd saved for Christmas presents, but it ought to be enough.

'How much money do you have?' she asked Callum.

He checked his wallet. 'Forty,' he said. 'Was saving for a new game.'

'That's loads,' Sophie said happily.

'Can we have two singles to Skipton, please?' she said to the man behind the glass once they'd got to the front. She spotted a phone booth and turned to Callum. 'Can we call my dad? Our parents will be going crazy with worry.'

'We can't risk it. We don't know if the police are monitoring their phone lines—'

The man pushed the tickets through to Sophie. He glanced at the screen. 'You'd better hurry. Last train leaves from platform five in two minutes' time.'

Sophie called out, 'Thanks!' without looking back as

she ran after Callum, as fast as she could, to platform five. The station was busy, and she skidded as she dodged around hurrying men and women, almost tripping over a dog lead.

'Come on, you two,' yelled the guard on platform five. Sophie put on another desperate burst of speed. Callum's long legs scissored along the platform. He leapt through the doors, reached back, grabbed Sophie's arm and jerked her through after him. The doors closed and the guard's whistle rang in Sophie's ears and she collapsed, panting for breath, on the nearest seat. Callum dropped down next to her. Sophie looked out of the window – just in time to see Hudges run on to the platform. She pointed, still too out of breath to talk. Hudges was gesticulating as he spoke to the guard, and the guard was shaking his head, looking at their train.

'How did he know we were here?' Sophie managed finally. It was like a nightmare! Maybe he was a witch hunter after all.

Callum shook his head – then his expression froze. 'The computer.' He dropped his head in his hands. 'I left the page open, it showed the train timetable!'

Not only did Hudges know they were leaving, he knew where they were heading too!

Sophie paced up and down the carriage and checked her watch. It was ten in the evening, but when she looked out of the window the snow that spread over the hills made the countryside seem almost as bright as day.

They were the only people left in the carriage.

Callum leaned against the glass, pressing his face up close.

'It's been a whole day,' he muttered to himself. 'Poor Katy. I wonder how she's feeling.'

Sophie patted him on the shoulder. 'I bet she's feeling sure that you won't abandon her. We can do this, Callum. We're going to rescue them.'

'If Hudges doesn't manage to stop us first.' Callum gnawed his nails.

'We've got past him once and we'll do it again.' Sophie grinned at his reflection in the glass. 'I'm a witch, you're a geek. Together, we're unstoppable!'

Callum snorted a reluctant laugh, just as the train

pulled in to a dimly lit platform. Sophie saw the sign for Skipton gliding past the window.

'This is it!' As soon as the train came to a halt Sophie punched the door button and stepped down on to the platform. It was icy cold and she shivered as the wind cut through her coat. Callum stepped down with her. Sophie turned to look for the exit, and her heart almost stopped. There were policemen by the exit, their high-visibility jackets glowing in the darkness. Callum's hand gripped her arm and she knew that he had seen them too.

'I think now is the moment for the witch element of Team Unstoppable to do her thing,' Callum said softly behind her.

He was right. The only way they could get past the policemen was by using magic. She thought fast, remembering the spell her father had cast that morning. Could she really conjure up a blizzard?

She closed her eyes and concentrated, trying to draw the Forces of the Earth together.

'Earth, water, wind and fire,' she murmured, 'bring the winter!'

Her Source tingled, but nothing happened. Sophie clenched her fists, willing the spell to work. Her forehead sweated despite the cold air. There was a gust of chilly wind, but there was no snow. Sophie began to despair – this spell was just too difficult for her.

She made one last effort. This time she relaxed, allowing the magic to come to her instead of searching it out.

There was a tingle in her fingers that spread all up her arms. A sudden frost bloomed on the platform, and a chill breeze danced into the station. The policemen shifted and rubbed their arms. A small flurry of snow blew across the platform. Sophie held her breath, willing it to cross just behind the policemen – and it did! Sophie gasped, realising she could steer the flurry with her thoughts. She passed it across the policemen's field of vision.

The trick worked. The policemen turned to see what was behind them. Sophie and Callum ran for the stairs. Ducking from shadow to shadow, Sophie made a last effort and a second flurry of snow blew up –

right into the policemen's eyes when they turned to look back at the steps. The policemen put their hands up to shield their faces. Sophie and Callum ran on tiptoes down the steps, into the underpass. Not daring to speak, they hurried along the dark tunnel. Sophie felt as if her heartbeat was echoing off the walls. They came out on platform one and sneaked through the side gate, out of the deserted station.

Sophie and Callum ran down the deserted, winding streets, into the town. She didn't dare look behind her in case the policemen were following. Their feet echoed from the stone-flagged pavements. The only noise escaped from the lit windows of the pubs. Sophie glanced left and right – and skidded to a halt as the words MISSING CHILDREN leapt out from a bus stop.

'Callum!' she called after him. 'Look at this!' She ran over to the bus stop, grinning with relief. If the police were still looking for Katy and Ashton, there was still hope. But the grin faded from her face as she drew closer. The two photos under the headline weren't Katy and Ashton. They were her and Callum! She gasped and stepped back. For the first time she knew how it felt to be hunted.

Callum's sharp intake of breath told her that he knew this was bad. But before she could speak to him, a woman, bundled up in a winter coat, scarf and hat, stepped into the bus stop. She glanced at her watch and sighed.

'Cold night,' she said to Sophie.

Sophie muttered a reply, keeping her head down. If the woman looked at the poster and then at them . . .

Callum tucked his arm into hers and steered her out of the bus stop.

'Not waiting for the bus?' the woman called after them, sounding mildly surprised. 'It's the last one, you know.'

Callum marched Sophie down the street.

'Don't look back,' he whispered. Sophie was shivering and not just with cold. Ahead of her, she could see the glow of a high-visibility jacket. Two policemen were pacing towards them, step by steady step.

'In here!' She pulled Callum into a shadowed alley between shops. She peered out as the policemen passed them ... then her heart sank as she saw the woman from the bus stop hurrying towards the policemen.

'Officer!' shouted the woman. She had a piece of paper in her hand and she was waving it to attract the police's attention. The policemen paused. The woman reached them and began talking quickly, pointing to the piece of paper. A gust of wind made it flap, and Sophie saw her fears were correct. It was the MISSING CHILDREN poster. The next second, the taller policeman turned and stared directly towards their alley.

'Come on!' Callum's voice cracked out. He broke into a run, down the alley. Sophie followed him. As she raced, ducking around rubbish bins and skidding on the icy, old stone flags, she could hear the police shouting behind her. One of them blew a whistle. Fear gave her a jolt of speed. They couldn't be caught now!

They burst out of the alley into a wide square where a church spire cast a long shadow. They raced across the square and down another winding road, lined with shops. Sophie risked a glance over her shoulder and saw a flash of neon yellow. Up ahead of them, traffic lights glowed – a main road. The lights were red, and waiting at them was a taxi.

Neither of them said anything, but they both reached the taxi at the same moment. Sophie grabbed the rear door handle and flung herself in. Callum followed.

'Hey up, what's the rush?' The taxi driver turned around, startled.

Sophie gulped for air. 'We missed the last bus – we've got to get to Bordley. The Duke of York pub.'

Callum nodded wordlessly.

'Oh aye. I can take you there.' To Sophie's huge relief, the driver switched on the meter and drove away as the lights changed. She forced herself not to crane over her shoulder, knowing it would look suspicious. But in the rear-view mirror she caught a glimpse of the police running out on to the main road. They doubled over, hands on knees, panting for breath as they watched the taxi drive away.

'Yes!' Callum exploded. Then, as the taxi driver glanced back at him in surprise, he coughed and said: 'Thanks. We thought we'd be stuck there all night!'

To Sophie's relief, the driver just laughed. She reached down to tap Callum's fist under the seat. It looked as if they'd beaten the police!

As they drove on, however, her excitement and relief faded. They were going down winding country lanes, with not a single light in sight. The snow was falling faster and thicker, the fields were like white bed linen spread out and the dry stone walls were capped with snow.

'Um, how far is it to Bordley?' she said.

'Strangers here, are you?' The driver smiled at them in the mirror. 'Visiting family?'

'Um, yeah.' Sophie winced. She shouldn't have drawn attention to them. But it was too late now.

'About twelve miles.' He added, 'Cost you a tenner.'

Sophie glanced over at Callum. She felt the change in her pocket. They hadn't got a tenner! Then she spotted something even worse – the MISSING CHILDREN poster was stuck to the back of the seat in front of her. She nudged Callum and nodded to it. His eyes widened in horror.

Sophie gulped. What they really needed now was a spell, and a good one – but she was exhausted, and terrified, and she couldn't think of a single one. She caught the driver's eye in the mirror and quickly looked away. To Callum, she mouthed, *I can't think of any magic!*

Callum raised his eyebrow and lifted his hand slightly. Sophie knew what that look meant: *You don't always have to rely on magic.*

Callum cleared his throat and leaned forward to the driver.

'What level are you on?' he asked cheerfully.

What was he talking about?

'Are you Elf or Warlock?' Callum continued.

Had he gone mad?

The driver raised his head excitedly. It was only then that Sophie saw the little elf figure dangling from the rear-view mirror. *Elfin Warriors!* That stupid game.

'It's the best game, right? I'm a Mage, fifth level. What about you?'

Callum whistled respectfully. 'You must have been

playing it for ages. I'm only a Summoner, third level. Hey, did you complete the Dragon Egg quest yet?'

'It's easy.' The driver grinned. 'When you know how!'

Sophie sank back into her seat as Callum and the driver talked potions, spells and skill points. *Forget about magic*, she thought. *I might as well be invisible!*

She only looked up when she saw electric light through the window. They were coming into a village. Sophie rubbed the window and peered out. It was tiny, just a few houses, and there, swinging in the snow, the sign for the Duke of York pub. It was exactly like in the picture.

'That'll be a tenner,' the driver announced. 'Hurry in, won't you – it's cold out there.'

Callum and Sophie pooled their money.

'Oh … um … we've only got eight pounds twenty.' Sophie felt very guilty.

The driver waved his hand. 'I'll take the eight and let you off the rest this time. It was worth two quid for the tips on defeating the Thorgratch Orc!'

'You're welcome.' Callum grinned back. They got

out of the cab. Sophie shivered and hugged herself in the falling snow. Callum beamed as he waved the taxi driver off.

'Nice guy,' he said, turning back to Sophie. 'What?'

Sophie rolled her eyes but couldn't hide a grin. 'I'm never going to be able to tease you about it again, am I?'

Callum shook his head. 'When we get back, you owe me a back-to-back movie session of the trilogy. Extended editions.'

Sophie would be happy to do just that *if* they got back . . .

NINE

Sophie shivered, hugging herself as the thick flakes of snow floated down in the dark. The houses around were dark, huddling as if they were just more hills. It was silent – so silent that it was hard to believe they were standing outside a pub. She looked up at the big stone building. Now they were closer she could see that the windows were boarded up and the sign was weathered and squeaking on rusty hinges. It was clearly shut. It looked as if it had been years since any Yorkshire puddings had been cooked there. All around them was darkness and silence, the empty moors.

'Th-this is spooky,' she said to Callum, her teeth chattering.

While Sophie let Gally out of her bag, Callum jumped up and down to keep warm. The thump of his feet landing sounded like an avalanche to Sophie. 'Let's hurry up and find them!'

'But how?' Sophie looked around at the shuttered cottages hunkered down in the snow. It looked completely deserted. 'There's no one to ask ... if only we had a Witch Hunter's Bloodhound.'

'Well, can't you make one?' Callum asked.

'I could try.' Sophie shrugged. 'What have we got to lose?'

Gally jumped on to a hedge and started pulling at the tiny branches, covering himself in snow as he did.

'Brilliant work, Gally!' said Sophie. 'This is hazel,' she explained to Callum, breaking a twig off. 'My dad said hazel is really good for *finding* spells, that's why they use it in dowsing rods. So that could be the pointer. Now we just need something for it to hang from.' She made a face and Callum echoed it. It wasn't going to be easy.

Sophie thought of the daisy that had formed in the candle wax. The daisy earring she'd put in Katy's friendship bracelet was gold, because gold protected witch hunters from witch spells. Magnets protected witches from witch hunters ... and the Bloodhound was a kind of compass.

'Maybe a compass with gold at its heart would point to witch hunters,' she said. 'Only we haven't got any gold, of course.'

'Yeah we have,' said Callum, a grin crossing his face. He reached into his pocket and pulled out his headphones. 'These were my birthday present – I wanted really good ones.' Callum opened the case. 'Gold transmits sound really well.'

'That's amazing!' Sophie's mouth fell open as Callum showed her the gold-plated headphone jack. 'So if we tie the hazel twig to the headphone wire ...' She took the headphones from Callum and knotted the two together. 'And now I just need some really clever magic.'

She let the twig dangle from the headphones. It turned and spun, but she knew it wasn't a real Bloodhound . . . yet.

'Forces of the Earth,' she murmured, concentrating on the twig as it turned this way and that. 'Earth, water, wind and fire. Lend your strength and show us the way to the people we want to find.'

She thought as hard as she could of Katy and Ashton. She imagined their faces before her, their green eyes and dark hair, Katy's pretty smile and Ashton's mischievous grin. Where were they now? Everything in her longed to see them again . . . and, as if it felt her longing, the twig tugged forward.

'It's moving on its own!' Callum gasped.

Sophie opened her eyes. The twig was quivering, pointing down the winding, snowy street.

'Let's go!'

Whichever way the twig pointed, that was the direction they ran. The snow made everything silent as if it were muffled under a big white duvet. There seemed to be only one main road in the village, and the twig led them straight down it, between cottages that seemed deserted. Sophie noticed that there weren't even any cars about. Perhaps no one lived here in the winter, she thought.

Sophie stopped as the road left the electric light and headed out into the darkness.

'We're going out of the village now,' she said.

Callum nodded, and folded his arms tightly. 'Onward,' he muttered.

Sophie, hoping that the makeshift Bloodhound was reliable, stepped out into the gloom. Strange rocks loomed out of the darkness, black against the snowy fields.

They walked in silence for what seemed like a long time, before Sophie noticed the Bloodhound twisting to the right.

'There's a lane . . .'

It was more of a track that led up the side of the hill. The mud was frozen hard into ruts, and Sophie and Callum almost had to climb along it. It was pretty mountainous for poor Gally, so Sophie picked him up and put him in her pocket.

'There's a cottage!' shouted Callum.

The Bloodhound pointed towards it. As quietly as they could, they opened the gate and tiptoed down the path. It was totally silent, except for the soft whisper of falling snow and the loud squeaking of the fresh snow under Sophie and Callum's shoes. Sophie winced at the noise and tried to tread more softly.

There were no curtains. Hopefully, that meant no one was living there. Callum straightened up by the window and pressed his face to the glass. Remembering the torch on her key ring, Sophie turned it on and flashed the beam inside the cottage.

It had been ransacked, just like the Gibsons' house. The table was overturned, and chairs were scattered and splintered. A bird cage lay on the floor, the door open. Books, their pages curling like pathetic fingers reaching for help, were everywhere. A huge picture above the fireplace was askew.

Sophie raised an eyebrow at Callum. What did it mean? Had the witch hunters been looking for Robert and Angelica here not so long ago? Her makeshift Bloodhound certainly thought there were witch hunters in here.

The end of the twig was tapping at the window. Gally jumped on to the ledge, also looking inside. Sophie noticed the layer of dust and dead insects on the inside windowsill. The place certainly looked deserted.

Her finger slipped off the torch and the beam cut out. In the sudden darkness, she saw a faint light coming through the cracks in the door. Callum nudged her at the same moment and pointed at it.

Sophie gulped. Someone was definitely home. Did she dare find out who?

Callum began creeping around the side of the house. Sophie followed him. It wasn't long until they came across an empty window frame. The wood was rotten with age and the glass had long ago fallen out into the flowerbed below the window. It was a small space, but Sophie thought she could squeeze through. She gestured to Callum, who nodded and bent to give her a leg up.

Inside was as dark and as cold as outside. Sophie screwed up her courage, trying not to imagine tumbling through the window, right into the arms of a witch hunter. Gally scampered over the threshold first, then climbed back up to her, tilting his head for her to follow. So she squeezed through the window, her fingers bruising and grazing on the frame, and fell forward into the room below. The landing knocked the breath out of her. She sat for a second, too dazed even to look up at Callum who was frantically tapping on the window.

Finally she managed to get up and let him in. Together they tiptoed across the creaking floorboards, towards the chink of light. Sophie stifled a cry as she stumbled against a broken chair. Callum caught her before she could fall. Sophie nodded to show she was OK, blinking back tears of pain – the broken wood had drawn blood. She reached out and very gingerly pushed the door. It moved slightly, and the widened crack of light was almost blinding in the darkness. Sophie blinked, then as her vision cleared she almost shrieked in excitement.

In the centre of the room were Katy and Ashton.

They were bound and gagged and tied to chairs, Katy's face was streaked with tears and Ashton had a gash on his forehead that was covered in clotted blood – but they were alive! She wanted to shout out, but she forced herself to stay quiet – there was no telling if Robert was still here somewhere. Instead, she motioned at Gally to creep in.

Ashton spotted Gally. His eyes widened in surprise, then he looked towards the door and finally saw Sophie and Callum.

'Mmphy!' Ashton yelled, through the tight gag. Sophie grinned with pleasure but put a finger to her lips as she pushed the door open. Callum hurried towards Katy and started untying her. Sophie did the same with Ashton, who was still trying to talk through the gag.

'Shhh!' she whispered, flapping her hands at him. 'Someone will hear!'

Ashton just shook his head and went on trying to talk to her. The knots were tight but finally Ashton was free. Sophie put a finger to his lips at once, but she couldn't hide her huge smile.

'It's OK,' Ashton's voice was hoarse. 'Robert's not here. He's coming back, though – we've got to get out quickly.' He shook off the ropes and grinned cheekily at Sophie. 'It's so good to see you, Soph. I wanted to kiss you goodbye before we left for the holidays. I thought I'd never get my chance.'

Sophie beamed. Ashton's eyes were soft and green and his lips were so kissable ... She leaned forward, but behind her Katy said in a mock-indignant voice. 'Um, hello ... Other people present ...'

Sophie laughed, feeling embarrassed, but in a good way. She turned to see Callum and Katy standing with their arms around each other. She hugged Katy tightly. 'I was so worried about you!'

'I can't believe you came!' Katy hugged Ashton too, still gripping Callum's hand tightly.

'How could we not?' Callum said, gazing at Katy lovingly. 'Now let's get out of here before Robert comes back!'

Sophie and the others ran out of the front door and down the path, through the freezing wind. The gate was standing open, but as she reached it, a gust of wind slammed it shut.

Sophie tugged at the gate, but it seemed to have caught on something and wouldn't move.

'It won't open!' she said.

Ashton joined her and pulled at the gate, but it still didn't budge.

'I don't get it. It was open a second ago.'

Sophie felt a sinking feeling in her stomach. This wasn't normal. She spun round at the sound of a car approaching. Then she heard a car door slam.

'Where do you think you're going?'

Sophie jumped back. Ashton put a protective arm around her. Through the darkness and the snow came Robert Lloyd. He strode towards them, his long coat whipping in the wind, an unpleasant grin on his face. His spectacles glinted.

'Run!' Katy shouted.

Sophie didn't need telling twice. She vaulted over the low wall, and Callum joined her. Katy tried to do the same – but she bounced back as if she had hit glass. She fell on her back in the snow, looking stunned. Ashton helped her up, and tried to get over the wall himself. But when he tried, he too was pushed back. Sophie blinked in amazement. It was as if there was an invisible barrier, one that only existed for Ashton and Katy.

She spun round as Robert came closer. He clapped his hands together and rubbed them, grinning as he looked at Ashton and Katy. His smug expression made Sophie furious.

'Leave them alone!' she screamed at him.

Robert only grinned wider. 'Can't do that, I'm afraid. You see, I need the Gibson children.' He stood smirking, the snowflakes whirling past him dizzyingly until it was hard to tell if he was near or far away. 'The chief of the witch hunters was not very pleased at the Gibson treachery. Not at all. If I hand over Ashton and Katy, he'll be so grateful that he'll accept me back into the community.' He shivered, as if thinking of it gave him deep pleasure.

'You're an idiot,' said Sophie scornfully. 'They promised you that last time, didn't they?'

'Oh but this time,' Robert hissed, his eyes staring at her, filled with hatred, 'it's different. This time they came to me.'

'You're lying,' Callum spoke up, but his shaky voice told Sophie he wasn't confident. 'What would they want with Ashton and Katy?'

Robert leaned against the wall. Sophie didn't like the gloating tone in his voice. 'Lucky little Katy has a choice: to do her duty and marry Tristan Blackwood on her sixteenth birthday, as their parents always intended . . . '

Sophie gasped, remembering Katy's scratched out name in the family tree.

' . . . or die.' Robert smiled.

Sophie reached out to steady herself on the wall. Her head spun and she felt sick.

'Katy's only thirteen,' Callum frowned. 'She's not allowed to marry anyone!'

Three years was a long time. Surely Katy could just agree to marry Tristan Blackwood for the time being? They'd be able to free her before the three years were up. Surely.

But Katy looked sad. She clearly knew more than Sophie did. 'They want an official betrothal?' Katy asked Robert. 'Now?'

'That's right.' Robert straightened up, looming above them. 'And once the promise is made, there's no going back. The anointing oil seeps down deep into each of them, sets their betrothal in their blood and bone.'

Katy's figure seemed to shrink as Robert's grew. Sophie could see her shivering and tears filled her eyes.

'If she breaks the promise so solemnly made, every ounce of her that is witch hunter will be destroyed, disintegrated, dismantled. Madness and death are the consequences.'

'Like being demagicked,' Sophie whispered in horror.

'Exactly like that. Once again, her choice is simple . . . death or Tristan Blackwood.' Robert's teeth flashed stark bone white as he grinned.

Sophie was speechless.

Katy looked at Callum. Tears were streaming down her face. 'Oh, Callum! I don't want to be with him, I love you, but . . .'

Callum was pale and he was clenching his fists. 'You've got to do it, Katy,' he mumbled. Sophie could hear the tears in his voice but he was trying to remain strong.

'Well said,' Robert hissed.

'Shut up!' Callum growled. 'Katy, of *course* you've got to do it.'

Katy swallowed, and nodded slowly. 'I know. But I'll always love you, Callum.'

'I'll always love you too.' Callum's voice was stony, but Sophie could see the tears rolling down his cheeks.

Katy said no more, but she nodded at Robert.

His smile widened. 'Good choice,' he said, and the gate slammed open.

Ashton and Katy marched stiffly to the Land Rover. Sophie could tell they weren't moving themselves – it was magic that was forcing them forward.

'What do you need Ashton for?' she shouted after them. 'Why can't he stay with us?'

Robert Lloyd grinned again. 'None of your business, witch. But you should say your goodbyes now.'

Ashton's eyes turned towards her longingly, then he was inside the car and the heavy metal slam cut them off from each other. Was this the last time she was going to see Ashton – ever? Did he have some witch hunter girl lined up for him too? Sophie made to run forward but Callum grabbed her arm.

117

'You won't get away with this!' she shouted at the car. 'We'll stop you!'

Robert rolled down the window and looked out. 'Good luck with that,' he sneered. 'You might want to start with taking shelter. If it keeps on snowing like this, the police won't find you till the spring.'

The Land Rover drove off with a roar and a flurry of snow – leaving Sophie colder inside than out. Robert was right. Without shelter, they wouldn't have a chance of helping Katy and Ashton escape. They'd be dead themselves, frozen to death. The snow whirled down in a crazy dance.

Ashton was heading to some unknown fate. Katy was going to marry someone else.

And there was nothing they could do to stop it.

TEN

Sophie felt as if they had been trudging for hours along the snowy road.

Her crunching footsteps beat out a sad rhythm, the snow writhing and whirling in her exhausted eyes. She didn't even have the energy to cry. Her mind and heart felt as numb as her aching legs.

Katy and Ashton were gone.

Callum's arm stopped her just as she was about to fall asleep on her feet. Sophie steadied herself on him.

'Sophie, we can't go on in this cold. Can you make a fire?'

'I'll t-t-try.'

They crouched down in the shelter of a wall and Sophie rubbed her hands together. She thought of the twig in the Bloodhound, and pulled it out. Using the headphone wire to rub against the twig, she tried to create a tiny amount of friction.

'Forces of the Earth, make this twig burn bright!' she whispered. She needed this to work. She couldn't tell if her Source was shining, it was too dark and its light was too feeble. She rubbed and rubbed again until her fingers hurt. Finally, the twig sputtered into a weak flame, hardly brighter than a match. Sophie and Callum huddled down in front of the fire. Sophie breathed on it gently, trying to coax it into stronger flames.

Sophie let Gally cosy up to the fire. She felt in the lining of her bag and found a peanut. She gave it to Gally and the squirrel devoured it in one gulp. Sophie stroked him. She always found her familiar so sooth-ing . . . but this time it wasn't enough.

Gally fanned the fire with his tail, then scampered away into the snow. When he came back he was carrying more kindling. Sophie gratefully fed it into the fire. With her magic and Gally's help, she managed to build it up so it gave just enough heat to keep them from freezing.

'I just can't believe it.' Callum was crouching, head resting on his arms as he gazed gloomily into the fire. 'I didn't even know about witches and witch hunters until a couple of weeks ago. And now Katy's gone for ever.'

'Not for ever,' Sophie said firmly. 'We're going to find them.' She tried not to shudder as she thought about Robert's threat: 'Say your goodbyes now.'

'But how? It's all just so ... so ... big.' Callum gestured helplessly. He looked up for the first time. 'What's it like, Sophie? What's it like to really be part of all this? I mean, to be a witch? I'm trying to understand but it all seems so crazy.'

'It's ... difficult,' she said, thinking of all the danger she had faced in the last few weeks. But then Sophie remembered the spells that she had cast, the feeling of magic roaring through her veins, the joy of mingling her magic with Ashton and Katy's witch hunter magic.

Just thinking about it made her heart lift like a balloon trying to tug away from the ground. 'But it's amazing. There's nothing like it in the world. I can't describe it, Callum. It's just me . . . it's who I am. And I wouldn't give it up for the world.'

Callum nodded slowly. 'I suppose Katy feels the same about being a witch hunter.'

Sophie nodded. 'I think she does.'

Callum rested his head in his hands. 'It's hopeless,' he muttered.

'No it's not! Don't say that.' Sophie reached out to put a hand on his shoulder.

'Of course it's hopeless. Katy's about to be engaged to the heir to the most powerful witch hunter family in the world. I saw his picture . . . I guess it won't be so bad for her in the end.'

'Callum, don't say that!'

'Well, what if it's actually best for her?' Callum said miserably. 'Why would someone as special as Katy, with all her witch hunter heritage, be interested in a boring geek like me?'

Sophie sighed. 'Callum,' she said gently, 'you may

not know it but you are one of the most special people on this planet.'

And Ashton's another, she thought. They had to save him.

'Also, she's only getting betrothed to him literally on pain of death,' she pointed out with a grim smile. 'I don't think that kind of thing . . . ' she stifled a yawn, ' . . . makes for a very happy marriage!'

'Yeah,' Callum said quietly. 'You're right, of course. Thanks, Soph.'

'Hmm.' Sophie caught herself nodding forward and pinched her arm hard. The pain opened her eyes. By the way her fingers were aching she knew that the fire had got her circulation going again.

'Let's go,' she said, stumbling to her feet. 'We've got to hurry – every second counts!'

'There's a house!'

Callum's hoarse shout jerked Sophie out of her trance. She had been stumbling forward along the road on legs that were so numb and aching that it was only her huge effort of will that kept her moving. In front of her weary eyes, the snow-covered hills and roads blurred into one white mass. She blinked, and saw that Callum was right. They were coming into a village. Modern cottages lined the side of the road and mixed with old stone-built ones. A red post van was parked up on the kerb. Sophie realised it was dawn. The light had come so gradually that she hadn't even noticed moonlight giving way to sunlight.

A postman whistled as he came out of one of the cottage's gates. He paused and looked at Sophie and Callum curiously as they staggered up to him.

'What's this then?' he said cheerfully. 'Last survivors of the zombie apocalypse?' He took another look at them and added, in a more serious voice: 'Are you two OK?'

'We're fine,' Callum said. Even Sophie could tell he didn't sound fine. 'But could you give us a lift to a phone?'

'Of course!' The postman hurried to open the door of the van for them. Sophie could feel him staring at them in concern as they clambered in. The postman ran round and got in the driver's seat. As he pulled away, he was still throwing them glances.

'You look frozen!' he said, turning up the heater. 'Been walking long?'

Sophie leaned her head against the window, nodding into sleep as Callum answered: 'Yeah ... it was ... um ... we're visiting ... We got lost.'

Sophie blinked as they passed a phone box by the side of the road, but she was too tired to ask why they didn't stop. Callum's voice sounded blurry to her, the drone of the engine rocked her and she was falling ... falling into sleep. She made a last effort to force her eyes open. They were just turning the corner and she saw a stone building with a blue lamp outside. Across the front of the building was a neat sign: WAKEBY POLICE STATION.

Sophie jolted upright. They'd been tricked!

'Callum! He's taking us to the police station!' She tried to force the door of the van open, but it was locked.

'Let us go! Now!' Callum tried to grab the wheel, but the postman pushed him away.

'Oi, calm down! You kids don't know what's good for you. This isn't weather for runaways. You need to be back with your families.'

Panic gripped Sophie's throat. They couldn't go to the police. The Gibsons would be in trouble, and they'd lose the time they needed to free Ashton and Katy. She tried desperately to think of a spell, but nothing came to mind. She was too exhausted, and they were in a van, a metal box with nothing natural around to work with.

'We're not runaways,' Callum protested.

'I've seen the posters. Got kids myself. I wouldn't feel right if I let you head off into the snow.' The post-man turned the van into the police station car park.

As soon as the doors clunked unlocked, Sophie pushed hers open and jumped out. Her legs buckled under her as she hit the ground.

'Hey!' shouted the postman as Callum landed next to her. Callum grabbed Sophie's arm and pulled her to her feet. Sophie tried to run, but with every step she took her knees trembled. She managed only a few wobbly paces before she heard a woman's voice join the postman's, shouting, 'Stop!' behind her. The next moment she was scooped up by strong arms and a policewoman was carrying her back towards the station. Sophie screamed and tried to kick, but it was like moving in a nightmare – her arms and legs felt like limp spaghetti.

'Just relax and come into the warm.' The woman had a kind, firm Yorkshire voice. 'I'm Officer Cooke. You're not in any trouble. But we can't have you wandering around on the moors and catching your death, can we?'

'Leave her alone!' Callum ran after them, but Sophie could tell how exhausted he was from his voice. The postman caught his arm and steered him up the steps into the police station.

'Calm down, pet. You'll be all right in a bit.' The policewoman sounded quite unconcerned. They went through another door that swung shut behind them. Sophie heard it lock automatically. They were trapped.

Sophie huddled in a comfortable chair, wrapped in a blanket and clutching a hot cup of tea. They were in the policewoman's office, a pleasant, modern room with windows looking out and in. She sniffed. The officer had the same perfume as her mother – that seemed really weird, but comforting at the same time. Worry about Katy and Ashton churned her stomach – and yet she had to admit, the tea was the best thing she had ever tasted.

Callum paced back and forth in front of the door. Now and then he tried the handle, but Sophie already knew it was locked.

The door of the office opened and the policewoman came in, smiling.

'Feeling better?' she asked.

'No,' said Callum angrily. 'You can't keep us here. We've done nothing wrong.'

'Your parents are worried sick about you.' She frowned. 'I don't know what would make you run away, but there's got to be a better way to solve the problem than double pneumonia, am I right?'

Sophie managed a small, weak smile. Callum growled under his breath.

Officer Cooke sat down at her desk and picked up

the phone. She dialled a number. Sophie watched her nervously. Who was she phoning?

'Mr Poulter? It's Officer Cooke at Wakeby Police Station.'

Dad! Sophie almost spilled her tea. Suddenly she wanted nothing more than to be back at home, safe in the arms of her mum and dad. But then she remembered that Katy and Ashton were a long way from safe. There was no way she was going home without them.

'Sophie?' Officer Cooke was speaking to her. She held out the receiver. 'There's someone who wants to speak to you,' she said gently.

Sophie took the receiver. Suddenly her heart was pounding fast. Her dad would be furious.

'Hi, Dad,' she said in a very small voice.

'Sophie!' Her father let out the word in a rush of air, as if he'd been holding his breath since the moment she disappeared. Sophie felt tears prick her eyes, her chest aching. But her father's next words told her that she'd been right to feel nervous.

'What were you thinking?' Sophie winced and held the receiver a little away from her ear. 'You could have been killed! I cannot believe how thoughtless, how—'

Sophie interrupted. 'I know, I know, I know, and you can shout at me later. But Ashton and Katy are in terrible danger. They weren't at the house in Sheffield. We've got to save them.'

'Er no – you have got to come home!'

'We can't.' Sophie didn't dare mention witch hunters with Officer Cooke listening to every word, she might think she was mad. 'If we don't do any-thing, who will?'

'Sophie, you are not to do anything. You are a child, and this is an adult problem.' Her father's voice dropped, and she could hear fear in it. 'I warn you, don't get mixed up in this. I'll do what I can to find Katy and Ashton, and your mother will come and pick you up from the police station.' When Sophie didn't answer, he added, 'I'm begging you, Sophie. You must promise not to do anything dangerous.'

'I can't promise that,' Sophie said. 'Sorry, Dad. I just can't. Not while they're in danger.'

'Sophie, I am ordering you—'

Sophie put the receiver down, cutting him off. Officer Cooke and Callum were staring at her with wide eyes. Sophie swallowed. Her dad was going to be *really* angry now!

Officer Cooke cleared her throat. 'Are you OK?' she asked Sophie gently. 'Your father loves you, you know. He'd do anything to keep you safe. That's the only reason he's angry.'

Sophie nodded silently. Officer Cooke meant well, she knew that. She had a kind face – and glancing at her desk, she saw a photo of a pretty girl about her own age. She had a daughter too. Maybe she'd understand.

'Please,' she said, clutching the edge of the desk. 'Please just let us go.' Officer Cooke frowned, and Sophie hurried on. 'Our friends have been kidnapped. They were taken by a madman. He's going to do something terrible to them!'

Officer Cooke sighed, and sat back in her chair. She glanced at her computer.

'Was this reported to the police?'

Sophie nodded.

'Well, let's have a look, shall we?' Officer Cooke switched on her computer. 'I shouldn't be doing this, but if it will stop you from running again,' she added with a smile. She beckoned Callum and Sophie round so they could see the screen.

Sophie watched as a database flashed up. The tab told her it was MISSING PERSONS.

'What are your friends called?' Cooke's fingers hovered over the keyboard.

'Gibson. Katy and Ashton Gibson.'

Cooke typed, and the names flashed up. Cooke studied the entry for a moment, then pointed to a single word: found.

'You see? They're back home, safe and sound. And so should you two be.'

'It's wrong. The computer's wrong. We saw them last night and they were being held by Robert Lloyd. Who updated that?' She pointed at the initials. EH. 'Was that Chief Inspector Hudges? Because he's in on the whole thing!'

Cooke sat back with an irritated sigh. 'I'm doing my best to humour you, but this is getting out of hand.

You're making a very serious allegation against a high-ranking officer.'

'I know it sounds crazy, but it's true!' Sophie was begging now. She could see from Cooke's expression that she wasn't convincing her. 'Please, you've got to believe us. Please!' She felt as if the room were closing around her, as if she were suffocating. No one believed them. They were trapped. And outside, Ashton and Katy were trapped too.

She couldn't stand it a moment longer. Jumping up, she ran for the door. She hadn't got two steps before Cooke caught her, swung her round and dumped her back on the chair.

Sophie burst into sobs of frustration and anger.

'Right. I've about had it with you two.' Cooke was frowning. She took Callum and Sophie by the shoulders and marched them ahead of her, out of the door. Her grip was strong and Sophie knew there was no sense in trying to wriggle out of it.

Cooke nodded to a policeman at a desk, who jumped up and opened a door behind them. Sophie looked around her. The room was painted a soft green, there were plants and comfortable chairs. Windows looked into the police station and out to the car park.

'This is the Family Liaison room,' Officer Cooke said. 'I'm locking you in here till your mum arrives. There's a water machine over there and I'll get someone to bring you sandwiches and blankets. I'm sorry to treat you like prisoners, but you've given me no choice.'

She backed out, and Sophie heard the clunk of the key in the lock. Callum slumped down into a chair, his head in his hands. Sophie was left staring at the locked door. Through the window she saw Cooke walking away across the station. She paused to speak to the policeman and Sophie saw her shaking her head.

Sophie dropped down into a chair next to Callum. They didn't exchange a word. There was no point. Sophie had tried everything she could think of and nothing had worked. She wanted to weep with frustration.

ELEVEN

Sophie flattened her nose against the glass, looking out into the office through the gaps in the blinds. The policeman was sitting at his desk, a half-eaten sandwich wrapped in cling film next to him, typing on a computer. It had been hours. They'd tried screaming and shouting and kicking the door. Sophie had tried crying. But nothing made the policeman look up – he'd obviously been warned by Officer Cooke not to talk to them.

Sophie felt in her pocket and found a penny. She rapped on the glass with it, although she'd long ago given up hope of getting his attention. Sure enough, the policeman acted as if he were deaf. Sophie kept on tapping the glass. *If nothing else*, she thought, *I can annoy him.* Maybe if she bugged him enough he'd let them go. She had to do something. Every rap of the penny felt like a second ticking away, another second lost, that made it less and less likely they'd get to Katy before she was married to someone she didn't love.

Behind her, Callum sighed in annoyance. He was lying on the sofa, moodily tearing a magazine into shreds.

'Can you stop that banging? It's giving me a headache.'

Sophie didn't answer. The door at the far end of the station had opened and Officer Cooke was walking through, holding the door open for another police-man. She stepped aside and Sophie saw who it was.

Chief Inspector Hudges.

Sophie jumped. 'Callum! He's here!'

The policeman just outside the door leapt to his feet, hastily brushing the remains of his sandwich –

and his paperwork – into the drawer. He nudged it shut with his knee and stood to attention as Officer Cooke ushered Chief Inspector Hudges in.

Callum looked over Sophie's shoulder and sucked in his breath as he saw Hudges.

'Look at them, bowing and sucking up to him,' he said angrily.

Hudges turned and looked right at them both. He gave a smug smile. Sophie gritted her teeth.

Officer Cooke led Hudges towards them. Sophie backed away and stood shoulder to shoulder with Callum in the centre of the room. She heard the key turning in the lock and the handle bent down. Callum swallowed loudly. Office Cooke pushed open the door and stood back to allow Hudges to stride in.

Sophie couldn't contain her anger a second later.

'See?' she shouted at Officer Cooke, who looked startled. 'This is him! I told you about him! Don't you think it's weird that he's here? He's in on the whole plan, I swear he is!'

'Sophie's right,' Callum joined in. 'He's working with the kidnappers.'

Officer Cooke looked nervous. She glanced up at Hudges, but his smug, confident expression hadn't changed. 'If I could have a word . . . ' He drew Officer Cooke to one side and spoke in a whisper. 'This is a matter of teenage melodrama. They're upset they were dumped by their boyfriend and girlfriend.'

With her witch hearing, Sophie picked up every word and snorted indignantly.

'It was me who broke the news to them,' Hudges went on. 'And of course they blame me for it.' He tapped his head. 'Basic psychology: I really should have been more sensitive.' He added, 'Perhaps I could have a moment alone with them, just to explain and apologise.'

'Of course,' said Officer Cooke at once. She gave Sophie a last worried glance and left the room, closing the door behind her. Sophie and Callum both took a step back. Hudges moved so that his back was against the door, folded his arms and looked at them both. His smile widened to show his teeth. Now it didn't just look smug. It looked scary. There was a tense silence. It was Sophie who broke it.

'Why did you do it?' she said, her voice trembling with anger. 'Why did you tell everyone they were safe?'

'Are you a witch hunter?' Callum blurted out.

Hudges' smile broadened even more.

'Oh no. I'm not one of them. But I know a good thing when I see it.'

Sophie shook her head. 'I don't get it. Why help them?'

Hudges paced towards them, hands behind his back. 'Because *they* help *me*,' he said softly. He stopped with his face close to Sophie's. 'You have no idea how powerful they are, have you? They're much bigger than you think. They're all over the world, in Swiss banks and Saudi oil fields, in Chinese aerospace and American crime families. They have long tentacles and a lot of power. How do you think I got these?' He tapped the pips on his shoulder. 'All I have to do is give them a little information here, a name there, a classified document there, and they give me a leg up the ladder in return.'

'It's you who has no idea,' Sophie said. 'You don't realise what you've done, handing Ashton and Katy over to them. What do you think they're going to do? Send them on a nice holiday?' She was shaking with rage. 'He threatened them. He's going to do something terrible to them – I know it!'

'Nonsense,' he scoffed. His eyes darted to the door. 'All that's happening is that a pretty young girl is getting engaged to a nice, powerful young man. Don't see what she has to complain about, myself.'

Callum growled.

'Just calm down,' Hudges snapped at him. 'I'm going to keep you here at the station, those are my orders. Until the ceremony's over and the deed is done. Once they've put on the anointing oil they've said I can get the credit for rescuing the kids. Sounds good, right? I might get a knighthood.'

Sophie shook her head hard. 'You won't be rescuing anyone. Robert told us to "say our goodbyes". I don't think they're just going to let them go.'

'You watch too many soaps,' said Hudges scornfully. But his face didn't look so certain. Sophie wondered if the Blackwoods had told him things he wanted to hear before . . . things that hadn't turned out to be true.

'You don't trust them, do you?' she said.

'Shut up!' Hudges turned abruptly and went to the door. Before Sophie could move, he had walked out, slamming the door behind him. She heard the key turn in the lock and his nervous footsteps hurrying away.

'Trapped again!' Callum groaned.

'Not for long. I've had an idea,' Sophie said grimly. She watched through the window as Cooke and the policeman escorted Hudges to the door. Cooke was clearly trying to impress him, waving her arms around as she pointed out the features of the station. As soon as they had left, Sophie jumped into action. She grabbed Callum's half-finished glass of water and threw the dregs on to the lock. Bending down, she whispered into it, 'Earth, wind, fire and water – rust this lock right up!'

There was a crackling sound as rust bubbled up all over the lock. The metal flaked and dropped off. Sophie waggled the handle and pushed until finally the door burst open in a shower of rust.

'Let's go!' she hissed to Callum, glancing around the deserted office. 'Before they come back.'

Together they ran on tiptoes to the front door. Sophie paused to glance around the corner. She could see Cooke and Hudges in the distance. Cooke seemed to be describing an extension, her hands gestured to new roofs and extra cells. Sophie jumped on to the grass and ran as fast as she could in the opposite direction. They had no time to lose – Hudges had said the ceremony would happen in just a few hours. A few hours to stop Katy being betrothed to someone she didn't love.

And they didn't even know where she was!

TWELVE

Sophie and Callum ran out of the car park on to the snowy road. At random, Sophie turned right and kept running. Ahead of her was a church, its long spire pointing into the grey sky. Tombstones leaned this way and that behind the stone wall.

'Sophie, wait, where are we going?' Callum panted behind her.

'Away from Hudges!' Sophie kept running.

'Yeah, but we could be running away from Katy and Ashton too!' Callum skidded on the ice and grabbed her sleeve just as they reached a main road. Across it was what looked like the centre of Wakeby. A small market was going on, a few elderly shoppers tugged their shopping trollies after them and stallholders stood rubbing their hands and stamping in the cold.

Sophie stopped, panting. Callum was right: they needed a way to find them. They needed a plan.

'We don't know where the Blackwoods live. We don't have our phones. And I've got no money left.' Callum pushed his hands through his hair, rubbing his head till his hair stood up in all directions.

'Me neither.' Sophie tried desperately to think what to do. She looked around. There was a road sign pointing towards the motorway. Three other villages were listed on it – Thursby, Bancombe and Casterwell.

'Casterwell! I'm sure that's where Lauren lives!' she exclaimed. She slung her bag off her shoulder and searched through it, looking for her notebook. Lauren had written down her address and number on the inside cover, with a smiley face after it.

'We haven't got time to pop in!' Callum said.

Sophie spun around, looking for a phone box. She spotted one on the other side of the market. 'Come on. Lauren will help us.'

She ran across the market, dodging between the shoppers and hurdling dog leads.

Sophie put her hands in her pockets. She had the twenty pence piece leftover from their taxi ride – barely enough for the shortest call. She put the money in and dialled Lauren's number. She waited, breathing hard. If only someone was in. If only Lauren would ring her back. She read the number of the phone box over and over again in her head.

Lauren picked up the phone.

'Hello?'

Sophie could see the credit was nearly out already.

'It's Sophie. Ring me back, please!' She gabbled out the phone number. The phone went dead just as she was saying the last digit. Sophie put down the receiver. She was shaking. She and Callum stared at the phone desperately. Had Lauren been able to write down the number? What if she hadn't heard it all before it cut off?

'I bet this is why Hudges took our mobiles. Humans are useless without them,' Callum said.

The phone rang. Sophie leapt for the receiver as if it was the last life jacket on the *Titanic*.

'Hello?' she said, clutching it hard. 'Lauren?'

'Sophie!' cried Lauren. 'What's going on? Have you found Katy and Ashton?'

'I can't explain right now. You've got to help me, please.'

'Of course I will!' Lauren sounded nervous. 'Listen, is it true you and Callum ran away from home? I saw something on the news about it. Your mum rang, she's worried—'

'And you mustn't say we called.' Sophie felt terrible not to be able to tell Lauren what was going on, but it was too risky. 'Please!'

'But—'

'It's a matter of life and death.'

'Well, I . . . OK, Sophie.' Lauren didn't sound happy. 'I suppose I've got to trust you. But this is really scary.'

'I need you to help me. I need you to google a family called the Blackwoods. Find out where they live and how to get there.'

To Sophie's surprise, Lauren laughed. 'I don't need Google for that! Everyone knows the Blackwoods.'

'Really?' Sophie couldn't believe her luck.

'Yeah, they're like royalty round here. They're a really old, rich family. They live in this massive old mansion called Blackwood Hall.' She sounded awed just talking about it. 'Part of it's a castle, dating from the Norman times. It's pretty close to my house actually.'

'Excellent, thanks!' Sophie grinned at Callum and gave him the thumbs up. 'So how do we get there? We're in Wakeby.'

'*Wakeby?* What are you doing there—?'

'Lauren! There's no time to explain! Just tell me!' Sophie yelled. She knew it wasn't Lauren's fault, but she was getting frustrated.

'Soph.' Lauren's voice sounded small and Sophie felt terrible. 'You're scaring me. But . . . OK. It's easy. You just have to get the number twenty-four bus. It stops at the bottom of the hill – you can't miss Blackwood Hall. It's the one that looks like something out of a gothic horror film—'

'Thanks a million, Lauren,' Sophie interrupted her. 'I owe you. Bye!'

She put the phone down. Callum grinned at her. Sophie grinned back.

'Let's go!'

They ran back across the market place to the main road. At the bus stop, Sophie traced the route. Then she stopped as an awful thought struck her.

'No!' She dropped on to the seat at the bus stop in despair. 'I spent the last fifty pence on calling Lauren. We can't even afford a bus fare.'

There was absolute silence as they stared at each other in disbelief. Sophie rubbed her forehead. If only there was some way to magic up money!

'So near and yet so far,' groaned Callum. He chewed his nail. 'Unless the bus driver plays Elfin Warriors . . . '

A car horn made them turn around. Sophie saw a small car had drawn up in front of the bus stop. The driver, a pretty blonde girl who looked about eighteen, put her head out of the window. In the back seat a younger girl, who looked about Sophie's age, leaned forward curiously.

'Hey, it's Sunday,' she said. 'No buses!'

Just their luck! Even if they did have the money, they would have no way to get there.

The girls looked at her sympathetically. 'Where are you trying to get to anyway?' the older girl said.

Callum and Sophie looked at each other. There wasn't much to lose, thought Sophie.

'Blackwood Hall. Do you know it?'

'Oh,' said the girl in the back seat. 'Are you working tonight too?'

Working?

'Er . . . yes!' Callum burst out.

'We can give them a lift, can't we, Fi?' the girl in the back seat asked the driver.

'Course!' Fi smiled at them. 'Hop in the back.'

Sophie didn't need to be asked twice. She opened the car door and jumped in, squashing up to the girl in the back, who smiled at her shyly. Callum got in next to her.

'I'm Shannon, by the way,' the girl said. 'This is my friend, Fiona.'

'Nice to meet you,' Fiona smiled at them in the rear-view mirror as she drove.

'I'm Sophie, and this is Callum.' Sophie wished she knew what job they were supposed to be doing. She planned to say as little as possible so she didn't slip up.

'Are you working in the kitchen?' Fiona said. 'You look a bit young to be waitressing.'

'Um, yeah. We are.' Sophie exchanged a glance with Callum. So the Blackwoods were having some kind of a party. And a big one, too.

I suppose a magic betrothal doesn't happen every day . . .

'Oh, you'll be with me, then.' Shannon smiled at Sophie, and Sophie smiled back. Shannon looked nice, she thought. For a moment she felt sad, wishing that things were simple and she could just make friends with her. But they had to get Katy and Ashton back. Nothing else mattered.

Twenty minutes later, as the car turned in through large, black, wrought-iron gates, Sophie glanced out of the window. The nerves were making her feel so sick. She swallowed, wishing she could get out and have some fresh air. The gates looked like a spider web spun across the drive, she thought.

'Are you OK?' Shannon asked. 'You look sort of pale.'

Sophie nodded and smiled, not trusting herself to speak. As the car drove slowly up the tree-lined drive, winding uphill, she slumped down in her seat. It wasn't surprising she was feeling so sick, she told herself. She'd never been more scared in her life. And she hadn't slept properly. She'd have to pull herself together – she didn't have time to be ill right now!

The car slowed, and Sophie looked up, hoping they had reached the house. But the towering, grim-looking buildings by either side of the road were just gatehouses. Two unsmiling men in suits were standing outside, and Sophie guessed they had watched them since the gates via CCTV.

Fiona wound down her window and smiled. 'Hi!' she called. The men didn't smile back. 'We're catering staff.' One of the men spoke on his walkie-talkie, still watching the car.

Shannon smiled at Sophie. 'It's OK. They're always really security conscious,' she whispered.

'Have you worked here a lot?' Callum asked.

'Yeah, every time they have a big do they need

kitchen staff and waiters. It's good – there's not much else to do round here for a part-time job.'

The man leaned in to speak to Fiona. 'Park up by the kitchen entrance. You know where to go?'

'Left at the fork,' Fiona said.

The man waved them forward, and Fiona drove through the gates. As soon as she did so, Sophie's headache worsened. It felt like an insect squatting inside her skull, sending out long legs of pain. They turned left and the car crunched over ice and pine needles. Sophie glanced out at the forest to either side. It felt as if something was watching her ... something evil ... or maybe it was just her headache talking.

A flash of neon caught her eye and Fiona braked, exclaiming in surprise. Sophie was thrown forward. When she looked up again, she could see a girl on a bike in front of the car. The girl was wearing a big coat and a cycle helmet, but Sophie recognised her at once.

'Lauren!' she cried.

'What – you know her?' Fiona said in surprise.

Sophie thought fast. 'She's working here too.' She jumped out of the car and ran to Lauren. Lauren looked scared and smiled nervously as Sophie reached her. Sophie didn't know what to think. Lauren shouldn't have come! It was dangerous! And yet it was really good to see her.

'What are you doing here?' Sophie said, making sure to keep her voice low.

'Well, you sounded so scared on the phone. I couldn't not come and help you, could I?' Lauren sounded defiant and determined. She tugged her bike over to the side of the road and Sophie followed. 'Um . . .' She glanced nervously at the car. 'What *are* you doing, anyway? Is it dangerous?'

Sophie took a deep breath. She glanced over her shoulder to check no one was listening.

'Katy and Ashton have been kidnapped. We think they're being held here. And we think they're in serious danger,' she said.

Lauren's eyes were wide and frightened. 'Hadn't we better call the police?' She reached for her phone but Sophie caught her hand.

'No! The police are in on it.'

'The police?' Lauren's voice squeaked. She looked at

Sophie as if she were mad. 'Sophie, you've *got* to tell me what's really going on.'

Sophie didn't reply. There was no way she could tell Lauren she was a witch and Katy and Ashton were witch hunters.

Even worse, she had no idea what they were about to see inside the house. Maybe Lauren would work out something strange was going on as soon as she saw whatever preparations were being made for the betrothal?

She shook her head. The ache behind her eyes worsened.

'I'm really sorry, Lauren. I can't explain it.' Her voice trembled as she saw Lauren's confused, upset expression. 'I'm sorry. But we need all the help we can get to find Katy and Ashton before ... before it's too late. Can you just ... trust me? Please?'

Lauren took a deep, shaky breath. 'All right. I'll trust you. But if I think anyone's in real danger I'm calling 999.'

Sophie smiled weakly. 'Thanks, Lauren. You're the best.'

THIRTEEN

The house was huge, built of grey stone with chimneys like overgrown oak trees, gloomy gables and a black flag with a golden crest of arms on it flying from the top turret. Sophie glanced around at the gleaming cars that were parked nearby: Rolls Royces, Ferraris, Bentleys. Fiona's battered little Polo looked rather sheepish next to them.

Fiona and Shannon came running up to them, carrying sports bags.

'We're late, let's go!' Fiona led the way around the corner to the back of the house and up two steps to a forbidding-looking door. A prim woman in black and white was waiting for them as they entered. Sophie glanced around. The corridors were painted cream, and she could hear the clatter of pans and chefs shouting instructions at each other from inside. She wiped her forehead, wondering if it was the steam from the kitchen that was making her feel so hot and feverish. Her head was still aching and now her stomach had joined in as well, churning away.

'You're late,' the woman snapped.

'I know. I'm really sorry, it was the snow.' Fiona hung her head.

'That's no excuse. Half an hour's pay will be deducted.' The woman made a note in her large leather-bound book.

'I wonder if Mrs Freeman has a sister,' Callum whispered.

The woman's head jerked up and she skewered them with a look. Sophie swallowed and tried to look innocent.

The woman waved Fiona and Shannon through.

Sophie stepped forward, smiling hopefully. The woman barred her way with a hand.

'You three are not on my list,' she said, examining the printout in front of her. 'Mr Blackwood ordered thirty staff, no more. I hope the agency doesn't imagine they can cheat us.'

Before Sophie could think of a word to say, Lauren piped up.

'Oh, we know Mr Blackwood only ordered thirty, but the catering manager sent us at the last minute. He was worried that some of the others might not turn up because of the snow, and he didn't want to let such important customers down.'

The woman looked a little taken aback. Sophie and Callum hastily chorused agreement.

'There'll be no extra charge,' added Callum.

'Oh. Well ... quite right too.' The woman made a note on her paper. 'Names?'

'Sophie, Lauren and Callum,' Sophie told her.

'You'll find spare uniforms in the locker room – follow Fiona and Shannon. Callum, the men's locker room is opposite. '

She stepped back to allow them through. Sophie scuttled past her, ducking her head to hide her big smile. Thank heavens Lauren had turned up! She gave her arm an appreciative squeeze as they went along the corridor, and Lauren grinned and blushed shyly.

Their uniforms were hanging on pegs in the locker room. Quickly they got changed into the black trousers, white blouses and white frilly aprons – complete with waitress pads and pencils in the pockets.

'I can't believe I'm in the Blackwoods' actual house!' Lauren fitted the maid's cap on her head and looked at herself in the mirror. 'I always wondered what it was like in here.'

Sophie opened the door and peeked around. The corridor was deserted, but she could still hear clattering and shouting. Callum came out at the same moment. Sophie covered her mouth to hide a smile at what he was wearing.

Callum rolled his eyes and tugged at his bow tie. 'Don't say anything,' he warned.

They went down the corridor until they found a

double door with a round window in it. Sophie glanced in to see white-suited chefs running back and forth, giving instructions and plates of canapés to more waiters.

'What should we do?' Lauren whispered.

'Mingle,' Sophie replied. 'And try to find out where Katy and Ashton are.'

Sophie pushed open the door and walked into the kitchen, trying to look confident. Almost at once, a chef pushed a tray of mini-sandwiches into her hands.

'Off you go! Hurry! Not that way, to the ballroom!' he shouted as Sophie turned around. He grabbed her shoulders and steered her towards another door. 'Go-go-go. The guests are hungry!'

Sophie found herself shoved out of the door and into an elegant corridor lined with beautiful walnut furniture. Portraits of haughty Blackwoods from centuries past looked down at her, and gilt-framed mirrors sparkled coldly. A second later, Callum and Lauren joined her, both clutching trays of snacks and drinks, and looking as nervous as she felt.

'This is beautiful,' gasped Lauren.

Sophie was feeling too sick to say anything, but she had to agree. Garlands of pink and white roses were looped up along the walls, hanging from the picture rail. She looked down the corridor. The garlands all led to two big, mirrored doors. The flowers were wound into initials: T and K, in a heart shape above the door. It looked like any normal wedding.

'That must be where it's happening,' Callum said, his voice trembling slightly.

Sophie nodded. And it could be happening any moment.

They tiptoed to the door. Sophie balanced the tray of canapés on one hand and with the other she pushed the door open a crack. Warmth rushed out towards her, and she swallowed as the sick feeling worsened.

She saw a huge room, lit by chandeliers. Men in dinner jackets and women in elegant dresses stood about in groups, chatting and laughing as they sipped their champagne. Waiters drifted watchfully about between them, ready to rush over as soon as one of the guests beckoned. Sophie could hear the strains of a string quartet from somewhere in the distance. But no Katy or Ashton.

She let the door swing shut, and steadied herself on the wall, her head spinning. Close by, she heard Lauren asking if she was OK. She made a huge effort and straightened up.

'I'm fine.' She managed a smile.

Lauren looked worried. 'Are you definitely sure something's going on? I mean ... I trust you, but it looks just like a wedding party to me.'

'Yeah, and the wedding's exactly what we need to stop. Let's get in there now!' Callum made for the doors. Sophie grabbed his arm.

'Hang on! We can't just run in like that. They know who we are, remember? They saw us when we were on Jersey.'

Callum groaned.

Sophie looked at Lauren. 'Will you go in for us, Lauren? If anyone asks after us, make something up, tell them we're fetching more canapés, or we've gone to the bathroom or something.'

Lauren nodded. 'And . . . what will you be doing? Or can't I know that either?'

Sophie and Callum exchanged a glance.

'Looking for Ashton and Katy. We've got to find them, before it's too late.'

Sophie and Callum tiptoed away from the ballroom. Sophie's stomach felt as if it was full of wriggling worms. She wasn't sure if it was from the fear that any moment a witch hunter might appear at the end of the corridor, or because she was really ill. She hoped she wouldn't vomit – she had no time for it. She swallowed, tried the handle of the nearest door and opened it gingerly.

The light from the corridor shone on to crowded bookshelves, an ornate fireplace, a huge wooden desk – but no people.

The next room was a long sitting room where all the pictures and furniture were shrouded in dust sheets. She opened a third door to see endless suits of armour and fans of swords hanging from the walls.

Callum tried the next one. Sophie sniffed as the door opened and a strange smell, halfway between incense and medicine, floated out.

'A ... chemistry lab?' Callum sounded puzzled.

Sophie peered over his shoulder. It was a big room with a massive wooden table in the middle that was stained with lots of different colours. Glass bottles huge and small lined the wall. Inside them were different powders, liquids, crystals and gels. The colours glowed and the strong smell made her want to sneeze. A rippling rainbow of colour floated and reflected across the walls and ceiling.

'It's a storeroom,' she said. 'This could be useful.' She went in, and Callum followed. He shut the door behind him, and turned on the light.

'Meteor crumbs. Granite dust. Mercury. Condensed breath from a familiar ... ?' he read aloud, scanning the bottle labels. 'Whoa – ground-up witch Sources!'

'Shhh!' Sophie interrupted him. She could hear something: whispering voices. Her heart jumped and she stood perfectly still, listening as hard as she could.

Callum pointed to a door at the far end of the

room. It was closed, but Sophie could hear the voices through it. Two men were speaking, and she could hear the grate of a pestle and mortar, and the hiss of a Bunsen burner.

'. . . pinch of python. That should do it.'

'You're sure? This is for the *Blackwoods*, remember.'

'Don't worry, I wouldn't mess up an anointing oil. Not for them.'

There was more rattling and scraping. Sophie heard a tap turn on and off.

'I don't understand why they're letting that Gibson girl marry in,' said the second man. It sounded as if he had moved a short distance away. 'They're traitors.'

'That doesn't affect the bloodline, though. The power's still strong. Besides,' his voice lowered, 'I heard Tristan wouldn't marry anyone else. He made a deal with Robert to find her, offered him reacceptance into the witch hunter community.'

Sophie stifled a gasp. Who did this Tristan Blackwood think he was?

There was more clinking and clattering, and the voice drew nearer. Sophie took a step back. 'Right, that should be it. Let's go and tell Mr Blackwood we've finished.'

Sophie and Callum hustled out of the door as quickly as they could.

As soon as she was outside the room Sophie gripped Callum's arm. 'We should try to contaminate the oil,' she whispered. 'Robert said something about the anointing oil – perhaps the ceremony won't work if it's not done properly . . . ' She had to stop as a wave of dizziness rolled over her. She took a deep breath and shook her head, trying to clear it. She knew she had to act fast. She could hear Callum saying something, but there was no time to listen to him.

'Ah ha!'

Sophie turned round as someone spoke behind her. Two young men wearing white lab coats were standing there. They had just come out of the storeroom. Sophie realised it was the witch hunters she had just overheard. Her head whirled. They'd been caught. They'd be killed—

'Are there any of those tasty prawn things left?' said the closest young man hopefully.

'Mini sausage rolls for me,' said the other one. 'You can bring us some, can't you?'

'Actually, we'll go down to the kitchen with you,' said the first. 'Don't want to mix with the guests in our work clothes.'

Sophie opened and shut her mouth, too terrified to make a sound.

'Um . . . yes,' Callum managed finally.

Not knowing what else to do, Sophie turned and walked away down the corridor towards the kitchen. The two men walked behind her, still chatting in low voices. Sophie knew they thought she couldn't hear them. She strained her ears to listen in.

'And what about the other one?'

'The Gibson boy? Oh, he'll be used up pretty soon.'

Sophie's mouth tasted sour. She swallowed, trying desperately to keep calm. *Used up.* The words echoed in her mind. She didn't know what they meant, but it didn't sound good.

'And what will they do with the body – once he's finished?'

The body?

Sophie almost tripped over her own feet.

'I bet it'll be up to us to bury him somewhere.' The man sighed, like he'd been asked to take the rubbish out.

They were going to kill Ashton! That's why Robert told them to 'say their goodbyes'. Sophie felt desperate. She had to find him and save him. She could feel her throat closing with the panic.

She grabbed Callum's arm. 'Callum, they're going to—' she whispered, but the men cut them off as they reached the doors to the ballroom.

'Thanks, but I'm sure we don't need both of you,' the young man said to Callum. 'This young lady can show us to the kitchen.'

Callum threw one last look at Sophie before he went reluctantly in through the ballroom doors.

Sophie could feel Gally wriggling around in her apron pocket, and put a hand down to try and stop him. If he got out that would be the end of her. The corridor seemed to sway up and down, narrowing and widening. She stumbled. Her stomach was churning and she was so hot, she could feel sweat running down her neck. One of the witch hunters was speaking to her but she couldn't make out what he was saying.

Calm down, Sophie, she thought. *Don't draw attention to yourself. Just act normally* . . . She took a deep breath and stepped forward. But the floor didn't seem to be there. She only realised she was fainting just before she lost consciousness.

FOURTEEN

. . . carefully . . . here . . . put her down . . .

Sophie groaned and rolled her head from side to side. Sounds boomed in her ears as if she were under the sea.

Just collapsed . . . some kind of allergy?

Can you hear me? Young lady? . . . hear me?

Her mouth was dry and her head was burning. She was staked out under a blazing sky in the middle of the desert. Ants were running all over her skin. Katy was screaming somewhere. Callum was asking if she could hear him.

You'll be OK. We'll fetch a doctor.

Callum, she tried to say, but the word that her lips formed was Ashton.

Did she say something? . . . couldn't hear . . . doctor . . . . . . think she's a witch?

The word shook Sophie. She made a huge effort and tried to sit up. She was in big, big danger.

'You lie down, darling,' said one of the men, pushing her back.

She had no strength to fight against him.

. . . be dead . . . ask Mr Blackwood . . . what else to do?

She managed to force her eyelids open. She was in a large, airy room, lying on some kind of couch. Through dazed, blurry vision, she saw the two witch hunters walking to the door. They glanced back at her with concern before shutting the door behind them.

Sophie closed her eyes again. Her head was pounding. Her skin felt as if it were on fire. *I'm dying,* she thought. She didn't even feel afraid, just so sick she was sure it was the end.

She felt something furry scrabbling across her arm, and knew it was Gally. He was tugging at her wrist.

Sophie tried to say, *Leave me alone*, but all she managed was a groan. Gally tugged harder, and Sophie realised he was pulling at her bracelet, the friendship bracelet Katy had made for her . . .

A sudden wave of coolness rushed across her, and her mind cleared. The friendship bracelet with the magnet in it that protected from witch hunter spells! He had turned the bracelet around so that the magnet was touching her skin. She felt better . . . but only slightly.

'Thanks, Gally,' she mumbled. When she tried to sit up, she swayed like a tree in a strong wind. She sat on the edge of the couch, knowing she should get up and run. But when she tried to stand, her knees gave way and she fell to the floor.

Sophie lay on the ground, trying to find the strength. She could hear the witch hunters coming back, their feet vibrating along the corridor outside. *Move!* she screamed at herself. But all she could do was roll under the couch. She pushed and pulled herself as far under as she could go. She watched through the gap between the throw and the leg of the couch as the door opened and the witch hunters' feet came in. She could see the hems of two white lab coats – and a pair of black trouser legs, and smart, glossy shoes. They stopped dead as soon as they were inside the room.

'I thought you said she was here.'

The voice was deep and powerful. Instinctively Sophie held her breath and froze. She felt like a fly trapped in a web, listening to a spider edge closer.

'She was, Mr Blackwood sir.' The young witch hunter sounded frightened and confused.

'She must have got better.'

'I'm sure she was a witch.' That was the other young witch hunter.

Sophie held her breath. They knew! As a witch hunter, he had sensed it.

'Not possible. Any witch that passed through the gate would have been killed,' said Mr Blackwood.

'Is there any chance the spell could have stopped working?'

'Hmm. I suppose if the boy's blood is running out already . . . '

Ashton! Sophie jolted alert. Her heart thudded as fast as running footsteps. He was here, he was definitely here, and they were using his blood to cast a spell. Another wave of nausea hit her and she had to stifle a groan. All she wanted to do was find Ashton and rescue him. But she had to get out of here before the spell killed her.

As soon as she saw the witch hunters leave the room, she dragged herself out from under the couch. Her hand clamped over the bracelet to press the magnet to her skin, and she staggered through the room, holding on to the furniture to support herself. When she finally reached the door she leaned against it, her head spinning. It took her long, painful seconds to get the strength to open the door and go out into the corridor. She managed just a few steps before she could feel the blackness coming towards her again.

'No', she moaned. *No, I can't faint. I've got to get out of here ... find Ashton ...*

She slumped to the ground, fighting against unconsciousness. It seemed as if only a few moments had passed before she felt someone's arms around her, holding her up. A voice was asking her urgently if she was all right.

'Lauren,' she gasped.

'Sophie, are you OK?' Lauren sounded terrified. 'Sophie, what happened? Did you faint?'

'Help me ... outside,' Sophie said, aware that her voice was slurring. 'Please.'

Sophie clutched on to Lauren as Lauren lifted her up and helped her along the corridor to the back door. As soon as she was outside her head cleared and she felt cooler and stronger. She took deep gulps of fresh, cold air.

'Are you feeling better?' Lauren helped her sit down on the wall.

Sophie nodded. Gally leapt out of her pocket and shook his tail, looking as relieved as she was to be outside.

Lauren gasped.

'That – what – that's the squirrel! The one from the sleepover!' She looked at Sophie, who could only smile weakly. 'I don't understand.'

Sophie was feeling well enough to feel guilty.

Lauren deserved to know the truth – but the Blackwoods weren't afraid to kill witches. Would they do the same to anyone who helped them?

Another wave of sickness swelled over her. She bent forward, her head on her knees, taking deep breaths, trying to fight off the spell's terrifying strength. It felt she was caught in a web of evil magic, the sticky strands tangling her ever tighter as she struggled to get loose.

'Sophie? You're scaring me. Should I call for an ambulance?' Lauren was bending down next to her, stroking her hair, panic in her voice. 'Are you allergic to something? Have you got an asthma inhaler?'

Sophie shook her head and managed to reply. 'It's not that ... help me get out of the gate.'

'Lean on me.' Lauren put her arm around Sophie and Sophie staggered down the path with her. She could feel the tendrils of the web tugging at her, but she forced herself to keep moving.

She raised her head and saw they had reached the gatehouses. The guards stepped out and blocked their way.

'Where are you two off to?' One of them raised his walkie-talkie.

'What's the matter with her?' The other guard demanded as they staggered towards them.

'She's allergic to peanuts,' Lauren panted. 'She had one of the canapés and didn't realise—'

'Someone called the doctor?' the first man asked.

Lauren nodded. 'We're going to meet the ambulance at the bottom of the drive.'

'Want some help getting her down there?' the first man asked.

Sophie's stomach clenched with fear.

'Can't do that, Steve,' the other man said quickly. 'Mr Blackwood specifically said not to leave the gatehouses.'

'It's OK,' Lauren said hastily. 'It's not far.'

As soon as they had stepped beyond the gatehouses, Sophie felt a rush of relief. Her head cleared and her stomach stopped spinning.

'I can stand.' She let go of Lauren and straightened up, steadying herself against a tree. She took deep breaths of the beautiful cool air. The snow sparkled and the sun seemed to gleam brighter through the trees. Sophie looked up at the snow-laden branches, glittering like phoenix tears.

'It's impossible,' she murmured to herself. No witch could get close enough to rescue Ashton and Katy. Just thinking about going back inside made her want to be sick. The spell was too powerful, too strong. Unless . . .

She swallowed, staring up into the web of branches. It was perfectly logical, of course. The only solution. It made Sophie want to cry.

'L-Lauren,' she said. Part of her couldn't believe what she was about to do. 'Please. You've done so much for me already and I am so grateful.'

Lauren's smile was puzzled. 'I don't even know what I've done, but you know I'd do anything to help my friends,' she said.

'I know.' Sophie pressed Lauren's hand in her own. 'And I'm so sorry that I can't tell you what's going on. But I'm going to ask you to do one last thing for me.'

Lauren nodded. 'Of course I will.'

Sophie squeezed her hand again, harder. 'In the corridor where you found me, there's a storeroom. It's the third door along on the right from the ballroom. It looks like a chemistry lab – you can't miss it. I want you to go in there and bring me these things.' She closed her eyes, remembering the list from that horrible day on the island near Jersey. 'Phoenix tears, granite dust, ground fulgurite, mercury and condensed breath from a familiar. You'll find them all on the shelves around the room. They should be labelled but phoenix tears sparkle. Granite dust and ground fulgurite just look like a grey powder. Mercury is silver – really bright, and it'll be in a jar marked "Poison". The condensed breath from a familiar will be in a very small vial, perhaps in one of the drawers. Have you got that?'

Lauren nodded. Her eyes didn't leave Sophie's face as she repeated: 'Phoenix tears, granite dust, ground fulgurite, mercury and – condensed breath from a familiar.'

Sophie made her repeat it twice more to be sure. She was expecting Lauren to ask what the things were, but she didn't. She simply gave Sophie a big hug, and said, 'I'll be back as soon as I can.'

She turned and marched off through the trees. Lauren's fists were clenched and Sophie knew she was screwing up all her courage. As sick and scared as Sophie felt, she couldn't help smiling. Lauren was the most loyal friend ever. Sophie was so lucky to have friends like her.

FIFTEEN

Sophie paced up and down in the trees, waiting for Lauren to come back. She tried not to think of all the terrible things that could have happened to her, but it was hard not to picture her tied up, imprisoned, maybe even killed ...

She chewed at her nails.

The sound of an engine made her jump. She whirled round, but it was too late to hide. There was a silver car coming up the drive. Before she could bolt back into the trees, the car had squealed to a halt next to her. The driver leapt out – and Sophie gasped with relief.

'Dad!' she screamed, running into his arms.

'Sophie!' Her father hugged her tightly, then held her at arm's length to look at her. Sophie saw with a jolt of guilt that he seemed to have aged since she'd last seen him. His forehead was lined with wrinkles of worry. 'Thank heavens you're safe!' He pulled her back into a hug.

'What are you doing here?' Sophie asked, her voice muffled by his shoulder.

'What are *you* doing here?' He sounded angrier than Sophie had ever heard. 'Your mother is picking you up at Wakeby police station!'

'We had to find Katy and Ashton. The witch hunters are doing terrible things to them and I thought no one was coming to help.'

'I promised I would help. I traced them here.' Anger crept back into his voice as he went on. 'You must never, ever put yourself in danger like this again. We were frantic. And this place is lethal! I can feel it already.' He glanced back at the car, and Sophie saw a horseshoe magnet hanging from the rear-view mirror. She also saw that there was someone in the front passenger seat.

'Aunt Angelica,' she gasped.

'I couldn't leave her home alone.' Her father frowned. 'I must call your mother. She will be sick with worry.'

'I think they are killing Ashton—' Sophie broke off as her father suddenly turned pale and swayed. 'It's the spell, isn't it? It's affecting you already.'

Her father nodded, pressing a hand to his mouth. Sweat had broken out on his forehead. He spoke with an effort. 'Car. Now.'

Sophie scrambled into the back seat with Rosdet. Her father got into the driver's seat and pressed a magnet against his skin. He shook his head. 'Like taking a paracetamol for a skull fracture. There's no way—'

Sophie could hear footsteps running down the icy drive. 'Someone's coming!' A second later Callum came into view, his bow tie askew and a frantic look on his face. He skidded to a halt when he saw the car, then when Sophie's dad opened the door to step out, a look of relief came over his face.

'Mr Poulter!' He raced up to the car. Sophie jumped

out to greet him. 'Sophie, I've been looking all over for you.' He turned back to Sophie's dad. 'You've got to help us. The betrothal ceremony's going to happen in the chapel, in half an hour. We've got to stop it,' he added, looking around. 'Where's Lauren?'

Sophie, looking over his shoulder, saw Lauren come hurrying around the corner. She had a tablecloth wrapped awkwardly in her hands, and Sophie heard the clink of bottles as she came towards them, stumbling and slipping on the path. She gave Sophie's dad a startled glance, but only paused for a second before running up to Sophie.

'This is everything,' she panted. She tumbled the contents of the tablecloth into Sophie's hands.

'Lauren, this is perfect!' Sophie counted out the ingredients, putting them on to the back seat.

'Let's go!' Callum turned to run back up the drive.

But Sophie's dad grabbed him by the scruff of his neck. 'You're not going anywhere! I'm not letting you, or Sophie, or Lauren go anywhere near that place.' He pointed to the car. 'Get in. Stay in. I'll rescue the Gibson kids.'

'No way!' Callum shook himself loose. 'I'll rescue my own girlfriend, thanks very much, Mr Poulter.'

Sophie's dad drew himself up, his face angry. Callum had never stood up to him like this. Sophie could see he was about to lay down the law. But then he staggered, the colour went from his face and he had to steady himself on the car.

'Dad!' Sophie ran to his side.

'What's wrong with him?' Callum asked anxiously.

'They've put some kind of spell on the place – it kills any one of *us* who gets near to it,' Sophie said. She was aware Lauren was listening with her mouth open, and tried not to catch her eye. 'That's why I asked Lauren to get all this stuff. It's the only way,' she swallowed. Callum looked confused. 'The only way for us to get in and save Ashton and Katy,' Sophie said, 'is to be demagicked.'

'De ... *what?*' Lauren asked.

'*Demagicked?*' Sophie's dad pulled himself away from her and stared at her in horror. 'Sophie, have you taken leave of your senses?'

'Dad, it's Ashton's blood that's powering the spell,' she said. 'He'll die if we don't rescue him.'

In the silence that followed, Sophie watched her father's expression change from horror to a settled, grim resignation.

'You're right,' he said. His voice weighed as heavy as the grey clouds that had started to gather above them. 'You must demagick me.'

'No, Dad,' Sophie said. 'It should be me. They are my friends and—'

'Sophie, I am not letting you go back in there. I am your father and I will protect you.' He looked very sad when he added, 'And if that means becoming demagicked, then so be it.'

Sophie couldn't believe what he was offering to give up for her. To risk madness, and even death … she knew her dad must love her beyond anything. Just as much as she loved him.

She swallowed and nodded. Her father collected the ingredients and walked away from her, into the snowy woods. He looked so lonely.

She could hardly believe what she was about to do.

'I . . . I don't understand,' Lauren murmured.

'It's OK, Lauren,' Sophie said gently. She managed a small smile. Then she turned and went after her father. Her footsteps crunched on the snow and questions beat in her head. Was she doing the right thing? She'd already made up her mind. She had to.

Her father was standing in a small clearing, ringed with pine trees. Among the giant trees he seemed a small figure. Sophie closed her eyes as a memory of the last time she had done this flashed into her head.

Her father's face was still shadowed with exhaustion and worry, but there was a deep determination in his eyes. 'Do it, Sophie,' he said quietly.

Sophie pursed her lips, not trusting herself to speak without bursting into tears. She crouched down and set out the ingredients in front of her in the snow. There was no test tube to mix them in, but the jar of granite dust was nearly empty, so she simply poured the ingredients into the jar one by one. First the gleaming mercury slithered in, then the ground fulgurite. Then the phoenix tears, each one sparkling like diamond. Finally, she took the tiny vial of condensed familiar breath. She shook the drops into the mixture, covered it and stood up. The jar was already beginning to fill with purple vapour – witch hunter magic. Sophie shook it. She couldn't take her eyes from her father. She longed for him to meet her gaze, give her a reassuring smile, but he was staring at the jar. She could feel the tension in him as the purple vapour seeped out from around the lid of the jar, snaking into the air around her.

There was one more ingredient. Sophie opened the jar, and pulled off her glove. Her fingers were numb in the cold air. She turned to a nearby pine tree, and scraped her knuckles down the rough bark. She winced as the skin grazed off. A line of blood appeared on her hand.

'And witch's blood,' she whispered to herself, and squeezed drops of her own blood in.

At once the mixture began to bubble and froth. Purple clouds billowed out of the jar, flooding into the air, shadowing the sky. Sophie wrinkled her nose at the strong smell of iron.

'By the Thirteen Families I swear it,' she began, her

voice trembling. The purple clouds were all around her now, cutting out the light. She could barely make out her father's figure. 'By the moon and the sun I command it.'

There was a rumbling like distant thunder and the trees swayed as if a storm were coming. Snow slid and tumbled down from their branches. The clouds changed colour, from purple to grey.

'Neither by dark nor light, day nor night, shall you ever again cast a spell . . . '

'Sophie! Mr Poulter!'

Sophie started and looked around as she heard Lauren's voice calling her. She could see a torch beam bobbing towards her through the trees, and then Lauren and Callum ran into the clearing.

'There's something weird going on,' Callum began breathlessly.

'The sky's gone all dark.' Lauren sounded on the brink of tears. 'Sophie, *please* won't you tell me what's happening? I'm scared!'

Sophie looked to her father, not knowing what to reply. They had to finish the ritual quickly.

'It's OK, Lauren.' Her father's voice, calm and strong, came through the darkness. 'Go back to the car. Everything will be all right in just a moment.'

'But the ground's shaking,' Lauren sobbed.

Sophie looked down at the jar in her hands. She'd told Callum she wouldn't give up being a witch for anything. And yet her father was doing it, for her. For her friends.

'By the Thirteen Families I swear it. By the moon and sun I command it,' she whispered. Though she could not see them through the dark clouds, she could hear her father trying to comfort Lauren and reassure Callum. They seemed a long way away.

'Never again shall you cast a spell.'

All that was left was for Sophie to say the name of the witch to be demagicked.

'Sophie Morrow,' she said.

She shuddered violently. Everything seemed very still and silent. It was as if the world were holding its breath, waiting for her to complete the spell. Her father gasped.

'Draw forth my powers,' she said.

'Sophie, no,' he said.

But she hardly heard him. It felt as if her voice was the only sound in the world, as if she were standing on the moon and speaking into the cold emptiness of space. She had to say it one more time for the spell to work.

'Draw forth my powers,' she said, and gasped as a terrible agony clawed through her, as if her heart were struggling to escape her body.

She'd done it. She was no longer a witch.

SIXTEEN

Sophie staggered and swayed. She could see her father running towards her across the snow, but he seemed to be moving in slow motion. The clearing spun, and she had a strange feeling, as if she were at the centre of the universe and all the planets and stars were whirling around her.

I must be going mad, she thought. How long would it be before she ended up like Angelica? Already she could feel strength seeping out of her, an energy she hadn't even known she possessed leaking away.

'Sophie. Sophie.' It was her father, supporting her.

'What have you done to yourself? I told you to do it to *me!*' He sounded as if he was about to cry. 'That was so brave.'

Sophie managed to steady herself on him. She looked down to see Gally leap from her bag on to the snow. He looked up at her, his eyes bright and wild, his ears pricked up. Then he backed away.

'Gally . . . ' Sophie reached out to him, but the squirrel flicked his tail and darted away, out of her reach. Sophie wanted to cry as she saw the confused, nervous way he looked back at her. 'It's me. It's Sophie. I'm the same person, I'm just . . . ' Her voice trembled. 'Just not a witch any more.'

Gally flicked his tail, gave a skittish jump and raced away into the trees. Sophie let out a sob.

Lauren was staring at her from the other side of the clearing. 'I don't understand.' She looked up. 'Where did the clouds go?'

Sophie looked at her father. He nodded.

She looked back at Lauren, and drew away from her father until she was standing without his help.

'Lauren,' she said gently, her voice shaking only

slightly. There was only one way to explain it. The same way her grandmother explained it to her. 'I am your friend and I love you. I have to tell you something.' She paused, and when she spoke again her voice was strong and clear. 'Witches are real.'

Sophie and Lauren followed Callum as he crept up the slope towards Blackwood Hall, Sophie's feet crunching on the snow. She was amazed at how different she felt: her senses were dull, like seeing and hearing through cotton wool. Gally wasn't beside her and she couldn't stop thinking about the fact that he'd gone. The world seemed less bright.

Callum paused behind a tree and Sophie joined him to peer around it. The wedding guests were slowly making their way inside a small stone building. Sun glinted on stained-glass windows.

'That's the chapel,' whispered Callum. 'That's where they've got her.'

'Are you sure you're feeling all right, Sophie?' Lauren whispered in her ear.

'I'm fine.' Sophie *was* feeling fine – at least, she

wasn't feeling sick any more. But everything seemed too light and distant. But she hadn't died, and she didn't feel like her mind was leaving her ... at least not yet.

She pushed the thought away from her. There was no time to worry about anything except saving Ashton and Katy. If she lost her mind after that ... so be it.

Callum was about to dart in but Sophie stopped him. She turned round and got out the vial of phoenix tears. There were only a few of the sparkling crystals left.

She pressed the vial into Lauren's hand.

'You two have got to get in there and stop the betrothal,' she whispered. 'Drop some of these into the anointing oil. That will contaminate it and stop it working.'

'And what are you going to do?' Callum was looking at her worriedly.

Sophie turned back towards Blackwood Hall. The front door yawned open like a mouth.

'I'm going to look for Ashton.'

Without waiting for another word, she broke into a run. She dodged from tree to tree and finally sprinted across the courtyard, hiding behind the shiny flanks of cars as she went. She hurried up the steps to the front door, and with a last glance behind to check that no one was following, she went in.

Sophie tiptoed through the house. The catering staff were already cleaning up the leftovers from the party. The garland had slipped loose, burst silver and pink balloons were on the floor, paper plates were balanced on the edge of tables, champagne glasses had rolled under chairs and the staff were making it all look presentable again. They had no idea of the horrible things taking place just metres away from them.

She opened door after door. There was no time to be cautious – this was her last chance to find Ashton. The house was a huge maze, and Sophie found herself panicking. There had to be hundreds of rooms.

She ran up the sweeping staircase, past portraits of grim-faced Blackwoods through the ages. Upstairs, more corridors lined with doors stretched out. Sophie took the closest corridor and went down it, opening

every door she could. She found bathrooms and stud-
ies, spare bedrooms that looked like they were being
used by guests, a luggage store, two laundry cupboards
and a room full of insects mounted in cases. Another
room seemed to be given over to mending clocks and
watches. She flung open the last door at the end of the
corridor, and stopped short.

There was a massive four poster bed in it. A large
TV covered half of one wall, and games consoles were
scattered around. Muddy rugby boots lay beside an
overflowing laundry basket. But what caught and held
Sophie's eye was a picture on the wall.

It was the same photograph she'd seen in Katy's
room, the one that had led them here. Katy and Tristan
Blackwood, arms around each other, laughing and
happy. This had to be Tristan Blackwood's bedroom.
She walked in, looking up at the picture again.

Blown up so large, it was easy to see the confidence
in Tristan's face. But he also seemed to have a genuine
smile. He didn't seem like a bad person ... and Sophie
knew better than anyone that witch hunters weren't all
evil. She found herself wondering how close he and

Katy had been. He hadn't taken down her picture when they split up. She hadn't thrown away her copy.

But he had had her kidnapped! What kind of guy would do that?

She heard a creak behind her and turned round sharply, remembering too late that she didn't have her witch hearing. Fiona and Shannon were staring at her from the door.

Fiona broke the shocked silence. 'I thought I heard someone in here,' she exclaimed. 'I didn't think you were the kind to go poking around in people's private rooms.'

Sophie found herself without a word to say. She winced at Shannon's upset expression.

'I'll have to tell the housekeeper about this. It's really serious, you know. She might even call the police,' Fiona said accusingly.

'No, not the police!' Sophie blurted out, thinking of Hudges.

'If anything's been stolen . . . ' Fiona left the sentence hanging and turned to Shannon. 'You stay there and keep an eye on her while I fetch the housekeeper.'

Sophie stood frozen until Fiona's footsteps had died away. Then she looked at Shannon, who was shuffling from foot to foot, looking embarrassed.

'Please, you've got to help me,' Sophie began in a low voice. 'There's something terrible going on in this house.'

Shannon bit her lip. Sophie could see she was uncertain, but at least she was listening.

'I know it sounds crazy, but there are lives at stake.' Sophie plunged on, hoping she was right to trust her.

Shannon hesitated. 'That does sound crazy. I don't want to get in trouble. Fiona said—'

'Please, Shannon.' She looked her right in the eye. 'My boyfriend is in serious danger – he could die! You know this place, is there anywhere you can think of on the grounds that seems suspicious some-how?'

'I . . . ' Shannon looked back at the door, then back to Sophie. She seemed to have made up her mind. 'I can't think of anywhere suspicious.' She took a step closer. 'But you don't seem like a thief, either. Listen, just go, quickly. I'll tell Fiona you pushed past me and

I couldn't stop you.' She smiled warily and stepped back so Sophie could get by.

'Thank you so much!' Sophie hurried out.

She was halfway down the corridor when she heard Shannon hissing her name behind her. Sophie skidded to a halt and turned round. Shannon came running on tiptoe.

'I've just remembered.' She drew closer, and whispered, 'I love horses, and I've always asked to see the stables. But they never let me. They're kind of weird about it. It's odd because they're pretty nice about everything else.' She shrugged. 'Maybe it's nothing . . . but there you go.'

Sophie couldn't resist giving her a quick hug. 'Thank you so much,' she whispered. She turned and ran back to the stairs. The stables! It was worth a try.

She headed out of the front door, and glanced left and right. The chapel doors were closed and she could hear a choir singing from inside.

So they haven't caught Callum and Lauren, she thought.

The path led down the slope and Sophie spotted a

track going off to the side. She went along it, hurrying through the snowy trees. After a few moments she came out into a clearing. There was a modern building in front of her. Sophie could see a horse box, but there was no familiar smell of horses and straw, and none of the stables looked as if they had animals in. It was definitely suspicious . . .

And then a security guard walked out of the main building.

Sophie was glued to the spot. She quickly put on a big smile as the man looked towards her.

'Hi!' she said, walking forward. She tried to act as if everything were normal. 'Why aren't you in the chapel? The ceremony's about to start – you don't want to miss it.'

The man looked at her coldly. 'I'm not a guest. My job's to stay here and watch the stables.'

Sophie was thrown, but only for a second.

'Mr Blackwood sent me to fetch you,' she said, as confidently as she could. 'He wants you up there now.'

The man raised an eyebrow.

Sophie swallowed. The man gave her a piercing

glance, then reached into his pocket and pulled out a small tin box with the Blackwood crest on it. Sophie didn't have time to move before he had opened it and thrown a pinch of the contents at her feet.

Iron filings!

Sophie's stomach lurched, and she almost turned and ran. A second later, she was glad she hadn't. The filings scattered and lay still on the snow. Of course, she remembered. She wasn't a witch any more. The enchanted iron filings wouldn't give any sort of indication that she had been.

She pulled herself together as the man was still looking hopefully at the filings.

'What did you do that for?' She scrunched up her face and tried to make herself look like a stroppy teenager.

'Shut up,' the man said.

'Whatever, I don't care.' She turned and walked away, her heart beating fast. 'But Mr Blackwood was pretty insistent, he said it was something about a guy turning up – Franklin Pewter, or Poulter or something. I'm just passing on the message. It's not me

Mr Blackwood'll be angry with when you're not there.'

She carried on walking and a second later, she heard the guard break into a run. He passed her, heading towards the chapel. Sophie stopped dead, waiting until she was sure he had gone. Then she turned round and raced as fast as she could back to the stables. She knew she only had minutes before the truth was out.

She ran into the stables. Along both sides were horse boxes. None of them looked as if they had ever been used. At the far end was a strange object. To Sophie it looked like a huge table attached to some kind of pump. There was someone lying on the table, strapped down.

She ran towards it. The table was shaped like a coffin, and there were ugly, cruel-looking spikes jutting out of it. A low, evil humming noise came from the pump. Sophie saw chambers filled with a dark liquid, and valves opening and closing, like a gigantic milking machine. Sophie broke into a run, faster than she had ever run before.

It was Ashton.

And it looked like he was dead.

SEVENTEEN

'Ashton,' Sophie gasped as she reached him.

He was lying on his back on the table, held down with leather straps. His face was as white as snow and there were deep, dark circles under his eyes. Sophie flinched as she saw the six needles in his arms. Tubes ran from each needle up to the machine, which hissed maliciously as it pumped up and down. Through the tubes ran a dark liquid. Sophie could guess what it was – Ashton's blood. '*He'll be all used up soon,*' the man had said.

'Ashton!' She shook him desperately. Ashton didn't

move. He didn't even seem to be breathing. Sophie tugged at the straps. They were knotted tightly and she couldn't unpick them. 'Wake up! It's me – Sophie.'

Ashton's eyelids fluttered. Sophie dropped the straps and cradled his head. Ashton mumbled something, sounding confused. His eyelids fluttered again and Sophie sobbed in relief as they opened and his deep green eyes gazed up at her. A faint smile touched his lips.

'Sophie . . . ' His whisper was very faint. Then a puzzled frown creased his forehead. He struggled to sit up, but the straps held him down. 'What are you doing here?' His voice crackled with urgency. 'You must get out, get out now. The spell will kill you!' He tugged at the straps, then fell back, exhausted.

Sophie could see he was slipping back into unconsciousness. Her heart felt like a bird trapped and flapping in her throat. How much blood could you lose before you died? The machine's hissing pumping was like gloating laughter. She raised her hands without thinking. 'Forces of the Earth . . . '

'I don't understand,' Ashton mumbled, forcing his eyes open. 'Why aren't you dead?'

Sophie's voice died away as she remembered: never by day or night, dark or light, would she ever, ever be able to cast a spell again.

Sophie tried to pull the tubes out of Ashton's arms, but they were held tightly by leather cords too. She looked around her desperately. She had to get Ashton free before the machine drained him completely. Callum's words echoed in her head: '*You don't always have to depend on magic.*' And then she saw them: the shears hanging from the wall of the stable.

She dashed across to the wall and lifted the heavy shears down. She carried them back to the table and stabbed and slashed at the knotted leather cords. They were thick, but eventually the cords ripped, and tore, and broke.

Sophie half lifted, half dragged Ashton down from the table. Ashton screamed in pain as the tubes broke loose, and the needles fell out of his arms.

'We've got to move!' Sophie helped Ashton across the stable, putting his arm across her shoulder. Ashton stumbled along, his head lolling. Panic clawed at Sophie's throat. She fixed her eyes on the door and doggedly staggered onwards. But Ashton was heavy, his weight dragged her down. She managed to get him just outside the stable door, and then he slumped to the ground. Sophie was pulled down with him.

'Ashton, Ashton, you have to get up, we have to run!' She shook him and tried to drag him to his feet. Ashton shook his head weakly.

'Can't.' He grabbed her hand. 'Go. Save Katy. Leave me.'

Katy! Sophie looked at her watch, which was now smeared with blood and mud. It was past four o'clock.

'The ceremony will have started.'

She sat back on her heels, looking around desperately. There was no one to be seen, no one to help. The trees surrounded them. She cried out for Gally, knowing it was useless: she wasn't a witch – he wouldn't recognise her.

But then Sophie saw some slow movement emerging from the woods.

'Gally?'

The little squirrel seemed tentative at first, then sped up, scurrying towards her across the snowy ground. The squirrel raced straight at her, leapt over Ashton and landed on her hand. He sat up on his hind legs, eyes bright and alert, watching her every move.

'Gally!' Sophie shouted. She hugged him as tightly as she dared, grinning widely. 'You came back!'

Gally flicked his tail, as if to say, *Of course!*

Sophie felt in her apron pocket for her waitress pad and pencil. Quickly she scribbled a note.

Dad. Spell is broken. Ashton in front of stables and he's too heavy for me to lift. Come and get him. Please.

She pressed the message into Gally's paw.

'Take this to my father,' she told him. 'And please, please hurry!'

Gally clutched the message and leapt down at once. Sophie watched him scoot away through the trees, like a flash of black lightning. She couldn't help smiling even though she was so scared. Gally loved her, witch or not.

She bent and kissed Ashton. He was almost unconscious, but his lips moved slightly, twitching in a faint smile.

'My dad's coming to get you,' she whispered in his ear. 'I'm going to save Katy!'

Then she leapt to her feet and raced away, down the path, towards the chapel.

Sophie's feet crunched on icy stones and her heart pounded in her chest as she ran through the trees. She skidded to a halt as she came closer to the chapel and saw that there were guards standing outside the main door. The three burly men wore dark glasses and had earpieces attached to their walkie-talkies. They stood in front of the main doors like a wall, glancing this way and that, scanning the woods.

Using the trees for cover, Sophie tiptoed around the clearing where the chapel stood. As soon as she was hidden from view, she ran across to the chapel and flattened her back against the wall. From inside, she heard the drone of voices. The music seemed to have stopped.

Sophie edged around the corner and saw Lauren

and Callum huddled by a small wooden side door. Sophie's foot cracked a twig and Lauren spun round, looking terrified. But as soon as she saw Sophie her face melted into a huge smile of relief.

'Sophie!' Callum exclaimed under his breath. 'Did you find him?'

Sophie nodded.

Lauren looked at her anxiously. 'Callum wants to just burst in. But there are too many of them.'

'I don't care how many of them there are!' Callum put his shoulder against the door.

Sophie grabbed his arm. 'Wait. Lauren's right. We have to be careful.'

She reached past Callum and gently turned the handle. Luckily, the small door opened without a creak and they sidled in, crouching down as low as they could.

Sophie found herself at the back of the congregation. In front of her were rows of witch hunters, some standing and some seated. They were all listening intently to Mr Blackwood, who was standing at the front of the chapel with Robert Lloyd. Robert was smirking, and Mr Blackwood had a hand on his shoulder.

'... I am delighted to welcome back Robert Lloyd, from one of our oldest families. Let his actions this day wipe out any unpleasant memories.'

There was a burst of applause from some of the congregation, but others muttered, and Sophie saw plenty of frowns. Nearby, one witch hunter whispered to another: 'I don't care how old his family is, they're all traitors now.'

Sophie edged along and stood on tiptoe to peer between the hats of two elderly witch hunter ladies. At last she saw what she was looking for: Katy.

She was dressed in a white wedding gown, with a veil wreathed in pink and white roses. Her hair had been swept up into an elegant sculpted do, and make-up made her look even more beautiful than usual. But there were tear tracks down her face, and her mascara had run.

A blond head leaned towards Katy, and Sophie recognised Tristan, sitting next to her in a grey morning suit. He whispered something to Katy and tenderly stroked a strand of hair out of her eyes. Katy gave him a venomous glare as she moved her head away from his hand. Then she turned and looked out into the congregation.

She saw Sophie. Sophie gave her a thumbs-up and a huge smile flooded Katy's face.

Sophie grinned back, placing a finger to her lips, then ducked behind a pillar as Tristan glanced towards her. It looked as if they might be in time!

EIGHTEEN

Sophie crawled towards the altar, keeping herself in the shadows. She gripped the vial of phoenix tears tightly in her hand. If she could reach the font before the ceremony was completed, she could tip them all in and spoil the anointing oil. Then the spell wouldn't work and Katy would be saved.

Luckily, everyone's eyes were turned to the front of the chapel, all their attention on Mr Blackwood.

Mr Blackwood turned away from Robert, who took a seat in the front row. He went towards Katy and Tristan. Tristan stood up, smiling proudly, and urged Katy to stand too. Katy rose reluctantly to her feet.

'Katy Gibson,' said Mr Blackwood. His warm voice was like the purr of a tiger. He placed a hand on her shoulder and Katy flinched. 'Your family may have been shamed in recent weeks, but what better way to cleanse you of their treachery than by welcoming you into our family?'

Sophie froze as he glanced into the congregation. It was a glance like a drawn sword. The few witch hunters who had been muttering fell quickly silent.

Mr Blackwood turned back to Katy and Tristan, and Sophie began moving again. Mr Blackwood brought out a glossy, purple ribbon. As he reached out for Katy's wrist she tried to snatch it away but Mr Blackwood caught it and held her firm. He began binding the ribbon slowly but firmly around Katy's wrist. Katy shivered as the ribbon wrapped around her like the coils of a snake.

'With this ribbon, I make you fast to each other,' Mr Blackwood intoned. 'Bound in word and deed, never shall you break the troth you have plighted this day . . .'

Sophie ducked behind the altar, and crouched down. She was only a few paces away from Katy and Tristan, but they had their backs turned to her. Mr Blackwood was intent on the ribbon, which he was binding in an intricate knot. This was her chance. She reached up and tipped the vial of phoenix tears into the font.

The oil in the font reacted immediately. Sophie jumped as it bubbled, spat and frothed. Small sparks of lightning flew up from it, and steam boiled over the lip of the bowl. Sophie grinned with relief. It was working. But then she looked up – and saw a hundred witch hunters staring at her.

She was about to run but took a last glance at the font . . . and her smile vanished. It wasn't the ointment that was fizzing, it was some kind of force field that covered it. As she watched, the phoenix tears slid off and shattered on the floor. She looked up and found Mr Blackwood glaring at her.

'Get her!' he yelled.

Sophie bolted. She leapt across in front of the altar, pushing past witch hunters who tried to block her path. She raced for the main doors, straight down the aisle. Confused, shocked witch hunter faces sped by. Someone rose to grab her, but Sophie was too fast. She dodged him, reached the doors – and slammed straight into the arms of a bodyguard.

Sophie shrieked and kicked, trying to get loose. The man's grip was as strong as iron. He lifted her and carried her back into the chapel. The congregation were on their feet now, shouting furiously.

'She's a witch! I've seen her before!'

'Saboteur!'

'Witch!'

'Let her go!' Callum jumped out from nowhere. The man holding Sophie grunted as Callum grabbed him and tried to wrestle Sophie free. But two more witch hunter men leapt into the fight. Sophie sobbed as she saw Callum in a headlock.

'There's another! Here, behind the organ!' A witch hunter woman called out.

'No, please!' Sophie recognised the tearful, terrified voice – it was Lauren. She managed to get her head up and saw her friend being dragged out of the corner by two witch hunter women. One of them slapped Lauren across the face.

Sophie sobbed out loud. 'I'm so sorry, Katy!' She'd failed. Katy was doomed, and now she and Callum and Lauren were going to be killed. She huddled on the floor as the witch hunters closed in on her.

'Let's kill her,' snarled one man.

'No, let's demagick her!' That was a woman in ruffles of pink and peach silk. Her wedding hat was askew.

'Yes!' The witch hunters all agreed. Sophie saw their white teeth flash as they grinned at the idea. 'What better way to celebrate a betrothal than demagicking a witch?'

Sophie gathered all her strength.

'You can't demagick me,' she shouted over the crowd. 'I'm not a witch any longer!'

The witch hunters looked at her in surprise.

'OK,' said the first man, 'so let's kill her.'

'Yes!' The witch hunters all chorused agreement.

'And her friends too,' hissed the woman in peach silk.

'They're not witches!' Sophie shouted.

'So what? They're witch spies. Die!' The woman raised her hand high. Sophie saw the glint of metal and gasped and flinched.

'Nobody is killing anyone!' roared Mr Blackwood, striding into the centre of the group. He pushed the woman aside and scattered the rest of them with a gesture. He scowled down at Sophie. 'Yet.'

He turned back to the witch hunters.

'Keep the children quiet. You can do that, can't you?' he said scornfully. 'When we've finished the betrothal ceremony, when Katy and Tristan are locked together for ever ... then you can do what you want with them.'

He strode back up the aisle. The crowd parted, and Sophie saw Katy sobbing, trying to pull off the ribbon that fastened her to Tristan. Tristan looked upset – he was trying to hug her.

'It's going to be wonderful being married,' he assured her. 'I want to spend the rest of my life with you, Katy. I always have. We're friends, and there is nothing more important than that. Can't you see how we could be happy together?'

'No,' Katy sobbed and shook her head. She looked up, searching the room desperately with her eyes.

'We'll grow to love each other,' Tristan told her.

Katy shook her head. 'Married or not, I'll hate you till the end of my days if you do this!' Sophie could see she was looking directly at Callum as she said, loud and clear: 'I will never love you, Tristan.'

Katy gasped as Mr Blackwood reached them and grabbed her wrist. He tied the ribbon around her and Tristan, layer after layer, knot after knot. Finally he stepped back.

'The true knot is complete,' he announced. 'Now for the final, solemn moment – the anointing of the bride.'

Sophie closed her eyes as he turned to the font, and stirred the liquid with a silver ladle. She heard Katy sob, 'No. No. No.'

And then an explosion rocked through the chapel. Splinters of wood flew through the air and stung Sophie's skin.

She saw the chapel doors burst open as if hit by a bomb. In the doorway, silhouetted against the light were two people. One she recognised at once. It was her father, a dull golden light shining from his pocket watch Source. The other ...

'Angelica!' Sophie gasped.

Her aunt stood tall and powerful, just as she had when Sophie first met her. Lightning crackled in her hair. It haloed her head like the branches of some magical tree. Her face was alight and alive – she seemed to have slipped off her coma like old clothes. Orbs of magical fire filled each hand, glowing and humming. Sophie stared at her, barely able to believe her eyes, a huge grin slowly spreading across her face. Somehow or other, her aunt had been remagicked!

Screams and exclamations burst from the congregation, splintering the silence. But the shock evaporated from Mr Blackwood's face, leaving fury as black as the heart of a thunderstorm.

Some of the witch hunters rushed forward, muttering incantations and holding up glittering instruments. With a single movement, as if they were one person, Sophie's dad and Angelica stepped together until they were shoulder to shoulder. A sweep of their hands covered them in a glittering force field. It glowed and hissed as the witch hunters' spells bounced off it.

'How did you make it inside?' Mr Blackwood hissed, staring at them.

'The boy,' growled one of the witch hunter guards. 'He must be free.'

Mr Blackwood whirled around, reaching for his jet staff, but before he could get to it, Sophie's dad lifted his hand. A blinding golden light blazed from his Source. The staff shot across the room and shattered on the far wall of the chapel. The witch hunters gasped. Sophie saw her chance as the man who gripped her loosened his fingers in shock. She twisted, and broke loose.

Angelica walked down the aisle, the force field glowing as the witch hunters tried to attack her. She paid them no attention, but gazed at Robert. Sophie was touched by the gentle, loving expression in her eyes.

'Robert, what have you done?' she said softly. 'They are children. Our sad story is not their fault.'

Robert was staring at her as if he were seeing a ghost. He laughed abruptly, with a sound like something breaking. 'How can you say that? How can you blame *me*?' his voice squeaked. 'As if everything that's happened wasn't your fault!'

'Robert, I—'

'Stay away from me!' he cowered behind the altar, and Angelica, pain blossoming on her face, stopped walking.

'Robert, our love—'

'Was all a lie! An enchantment. You cast a spell to make me think I was in love with you!'

'No!' Angelica's hands flew to her heart as if she was trying to defend herself.

'I am a witch hunter – a proud witch hunter, a loyal witch hunter!' Robert was cringing on the floor now. He tugged at Mr Blackwood's sleeve. 'Sir, please believe me. Don't cast me out again. Destroy her! Destroy her now!'

Mr Blackwood, a disgusted expression on his face, shook him loose.

'Finish your own dirty work, Robert,' he said coldly.

Sophie cried out as she saw Robert turn and rise, an orb of fiery magic blazing in his hands. The orb flew from him, directly at Angelica, and her force field vanished with a shriek. Angelica staggered back.

Sophie's dad ran forward. 'Angelica! No!' he shouted. But it was too late.

Orbs of heavy, burning ice flew from Angelica's hands to Robert. They smashed into the altar, leaving smoking holes, but Robert was no longer there. He had dodged, and now ran down the chapel, hurdling the pews and scattering screaming witch hunters, while a rain of orbs flew from his hands towards Angelica. Sophie ducked behind a pillar as the chapel filled with blazing fire, burning ice, huge boulders and orbs of water that hit the walls with the force of cannon balls. The stained-glass windows shattered, people screamed, pews burst into flame. Sophie, desperate to know if her father and friends were safe, risked a glance around the pillar. She was just in time to see a huge orb of fire smash directly into Angelica's heart. Angelica flew backwards, the orbs in her hands fading and disappearing. With a horrible thud she landed on her back on the floor. Sophie waited for her to rise, but she didn't. She lay perfectly still, her eyes closed, her hands open and defenceless.

An awful silence settled over the remains of the chapel.

'Angelica!' gasped Sophie's dad. His voice trembled. He raced to her side, and crouched by her, cradling her in his arms. 'No, no, no. Please, no. You can't be dead!'

Sophie was about to run to his side, when she hesitated. A strange tingling feeling was running all over her skin, deep into her body, as if something new was coursing through her veins instead of blood. She looked down at her hands in surprise. Her Source was burning the brightest silver, more brightly than she had ever seen it burn before. And then Sophie realised what was happening.

She drew in her breath with a shudder of delight and disbelief. It was impossible – it was incredible – but it was really happening. Angelica's powers were seeping into her.

Sophie was a witch again.

NINETEEN

Sophie stepped out from behind the pillar. She could feel her whole body trembling with power. She looked up to see the witch hunters moving down the aisle towards her father. They were battered and bruised, and one lady was patting out the flames on her outfit, but the fury and malice as they moved towards where her father crouched weeping over his sister's body was undimmed. At their head was Mr Blackwood.

Sophie clenched her fists and took a deep breath.

'Get away from them,' she said. She had the sense that she was keeping a lid on a building head of steam.

She felt strangely detached from herself, as if she were watching this happening to someone else.

Mr Blackwood's head jerked up. He narrowed his eyes at her.

'Well, well, it's the ex-witch,' he said mockingly. He glanced back at his followers. 'What do we call an ex-witch, do you think?'

'Dead,' said Robert. He was standing by the altar, and he lifted his hands towards Sophie. But Sophie was quicker. Almost without thinking, she raised her hands. Orbs of fire flew from them, and knocked Mr Blackwood and Robert backwards. As the other witch hunters tried to attack, Sophie – moving by instinct – swept her hands across her body. A glittering in the air told her that she'd created a force field. She felt surges of warmth as the witch hunters' spells broke against it.

'Good work, Sophie!' Her father was by her side. He clasped Angelica, lifeless, in one arm, in the other he held a bubbling well of water magic. Sophie felt his strength, rooted down into the earth like a tree. 'Get Katy. I'll hold them back.'

Sophie raced up to the altar, while around her orbs

and spells burst and blasted. She found Katy shelter-
ing behind the altar. Her face was smudged with
scorch marks and her dress was torn – but she'd managed to get the purple ribbon off her wrist. Beside her,
Tristan Blackwood lay on the ground, unconscious.

'What happened?' Sophie said, grabbing her arm
and sweeping a force field around both of them.

'I punched him.'

The chapel rocked with the impact of another blast
of magic so Sophie didn't stop to hug Katy just then.
'Where are Lauren and Callum?' she asked.

'They got out when the fighting started,' said Katy.
'Callum didn't want to go but I made him.'

'Great, come on!' Sophie ran for the door, pulling
Katy with her.

Ahead of her, Sophie's father walked backwards,
firing orbs to keep the witch hunters back. Sophie and
Katy staggered out of the chapel, into the cold winter
air, and down the steps to the path.

Sophie looked back as they reached the edge of the
forest. Her father was running up behind her, and he
caught her arm.

'Come on! There's a hundred of them back there!' he gasped.

Together the three of them ran down the path, through the forest. Sophie didn't dare look over her shoulder – she focused on not stumbling, and keeping Katy upright.

'There! The gatehouses!' she shouted, pointing as the roof appeared through the trees. Another burst of speed and she was stumbling from the path on to the tarmac of the road. She fell to her knees, the rough surface skinning her hands as, exhausted and breathless, she toppled forward. The force field had faded.

'Where do you think you're going?' growled a man's rough voice.

Sophie looked up to see the gatehouse attendants blocking the way, arms folded. Behind them, the gate was locked, like a metal spider web barring the way. Her head reeled with exhaustion. She knew she didn't have the strength to fire more orbs, and looking back at her father, she could tell he didn't either.

And then two small figures ran out in front of the locked gate.

'Hey!' Lauren and Callum yelled, waving. 'Hey! Over here!'

'Katy!' Callum called through the gate. 'You OK?'

'Still standing!' Katy shouted back, wiping the streaky mascara from her face and giving him a weak grin.

The attendants turned, jaws dropping. Sophie looked past Lauren as the sound of sirens stirred the air. Blue lights flashed through the trees, and her heart sank.

Chief Inspector Hudges had caught up with them. Now they had enemies on all sides. It was over.

The first police car screeched to a halt in front of the gates. More police cars backed up behind it. The attendants looked at each other anxiously. One reached for his walkie-talkie.

Sophie got slowly to her feet. She looked at Katy, and could see the same exhausted determination on her face. They were going to go down fighting. She clasped Katy's hand and Katy gripped hers tightly. Sophie's dad moved to stand behind them like a shield.

The door of the first police car opened, and . . .

'Mum!' screamed Sophie.

She dropped Katy's hand and raced towards her mother, ignoring the attendants. The gates barred her way, but the second person to get out of the car was Officer Cooke. She ordered the guards to stand aside and, with a wary look at the five or six cars blocking the drive, they did.

Sophie pushed the gates open, and threw herself into her mother's hug. For a warm, perfect moment she was in the safest place in the world.

Her mother shook her gently. 'Don't you ever do that to me again!' Her voice was choked with happy tears.

'I'm so sorry, Mum!'

Sophie looked around. Swarms of police officers were heading up the hill to the house. She could see the gatehouse attendants being led away in handcuffs, while another policewoman wrapped Katy and Callum in the same blanket. Their arms were wrapped so tightly round each other that it was easy for them to share.

'Where's Ashton?'

Her dad pointed to the car where paramedics were already attending to him.

Officer Cooke stood in front of Sophie. 'Let them deal with him. Give them space.' Her serious expression chilled Sophie's blood. 'I'm sorry we didn't believe you, Sophie. We looked into it further and well … Chief Inspector Hudges has been arrested. And we're here to arrest the Blackwoods, too. For kidnapping.' She shook her head. 'It's an extraordinary story. One would never have suspected such a powerful family … I don't know what can have driven them to this.'

Sophie exchanged a glance with her mother. She knew Officer Cooke would never believe the truth. They weren't going to be the ones to tell her that all this was to do with a centuries-old feud between witches and witch hunters. That stupid grudges had made them kidnap her friends, and kill her aunt.

Sophie looked over at Ashton's pale, limp figure in the paramedic car and vowed that she would spend the rest of her life trying to end the rift.

*

Sophie stepped away from the hospital window. She'd been watching Gally playing outside in the trees, trying to give Ashton some time with his parents and sister . . . but she couldn't stay away for long. And judging by the look Ashton gave her as she came back to the side of his bed, he didn't want her to. Sophie blushed. The Gibsons moved aside to let her in, and Ashton reached out for her hand. Sophie took it, glad to feel that some warmth and strength had come back into his fingers at last.

'I can't believe you've saved my life twice now,' said Ashton. His voice was weak but the mischievous glint in his eyes was back. 'And I've never saved yours.'

Sophie laughed. 'I hope you never have to, either!'

He grinned. 'Hey, the doctor says I'm well enough to go home now.'

'Home? But is it safe?' Katy asked.

Mr Gibson nodded. Sophie could see he had new wrinkles and furrows in his face, but he looked happy again at last.

'I think so. There's a lot of tidying up to do, but with the Blackwoods in prison, and Hudges and

Robert arrested too, I think we'll be safe from other witch hunters . . . for now.'

Sophie shivered, thinking back to the horror of that last day in the chapel.

'I'm so sorry about your aunt,' Mrs Gibson said gently. 'When is the funeral? I hope we can come and pay our condolences. She was a disturbed woman, but . . . well, she was married to one of us, and that makes her family.'

'Thanks.' Sophie swallowed. It was still so hard to believe that Angelica was dead.

'I still don't understand how it all happened,' Katy said.

'My father explained it. He said that when I demagicked myself, my powers went into Angelica, and . . . he said when she woke up she was like her old self, before she and Robert were split up. But then when Angelica died, her powers re-entered me.'

'So she's still alive inside you, in a small way,' Ashton said, gently pressing Sophie's fingers.

Sophie nodded. It was the one comforting thing that she could return to. Angelica's powers had made her stronger, too. It was hard to get used to it, to the new feeling of power living inside her. She hoped she would be strong enough to use it well.

There was a tap on the door and a doctor entered. Mr and Mrs Gibson stood up at once and began talking to him about taking Ashton home. Katy drew Sophie aside. Together they went to the window and looked down over the woods, to the distant turrets of Turlingham Academy and the even more distant sea.

'You know, that protective spell the Blackwoods put on the mansion should have killed you,' Katy said in a low voice.

'That's what my dad said too.' Sophie watched as Gally scampered from branch to branch, shaking the snow down from the laden trees.

'Most witches would have died in ten minutes. But you survived for like half an hour and just got sick. And ... I have a theory about why.'

'You do?' Sophie turned to Katy.

'I think there must be something in Ashton's blood that wouldn't harm you.'

'Really?' Sophie was startled. She realised Katy was hiding a smile. 'What does that mean?'

Katy glanced over her shoulder towards Ashton's bed, then drew closer to Sophie.

'It means,' she whispered, allowing the smile to break through, 'that my brother must like you. A lot!'

When Sophie looked at Ashton she knew that she liked him a lot too. It was hard enough being a witch. And being a witch dating a witch hunter was even harder. But being with Ashton, Sophie knew it was definitely worth it.

They'd face down everything.

Together.